I scooped up a snowball and flung it at Jude, then turned and headed quickly down the hill on my sled.

"You're gonna be sorry!" he called as he followed after me.

I didn't think so. How could any girl be sorry when she had a hot Aussie on her tail?

Also by Rachel Hawthorne

Caribbean Cruising
Island Girls (and Boys)
Love on the Lifts
Thrill Ride
The Boyfriend League
Snowed In
Labor of Love

RACHEL HAWTHORNE

HARPER TEEN

An Imprint of HarperCollins*Publishers*

HarperTeen is an imprint
of HarperCollins Publishers.

Suite Dreams

Printed in the United States of America.

www.harperteen.com

Library of Congress catalog card number: 2008928089
ISBN 978-0-06-168806-5

Typography by Andrea Vandergrift

❖

First Edition

For Anna Campbell,
advisor on all things Australian

Chapter 1

"So what are you and the main squeeze doing over winter break?"

We were definitely *not* going to be doing any squeezing. Although I wasn't ready to admit that yet. Not to anyone. Not even Mel, the closest thing I had to a best friend on campus.

We were walking home after finishing our shift at The Chalet—a fancy schmancy restaurant near the university where we were both students. It was a little after eleven but a full moon, the wreath-decorated streetlights, and the twinkling white lights on the trees illuminated our path along the snow-covered sidewalk. Our black ties and aprons were tucked into our pockets and our jackets were zipped against the brisk wind and swirling snow. My red knitted cap was pulled down low over my black hair, keeping my ears semiwarm.

Mel was a year older than I was, but she didn't hold my freshman status against me. Besides, after only one semester I was a mere three hours short of being a sophomore myself, having placed out of some courses and then carrying a full course load.

I was embarrassingly smart—at least in the world of academia.

When it came to relationships with guys, though, I was a total ignoramus.

Case in point: Today was the beginning of winter break and my first boyfriend ever was at that very moment flying the friendly skies, heading to Australia—without me.

I'd met Rick the day I moved into Wilson Hall. He'd helped unload my boxes from my parents' car, teasing me the entire time because I had so much stuff. He was a minimalist who boasted that he could fit his life into one box. He'd never met a single-purpose item that he liked.

We'd spent the semester hanging out together, being a couple. We lived in the same co-ed dorm, which made it convenient. We ate meals together, went to the library to study, attended football games, and had amazing make-out sessions.

I'd viewed the upcoming winter break—when studying wouldn't be a necessity—as a time for us to take our relationship to the next level, to strengthen our bond, to get to know each other even better.

But right before finals, he'd begun to question whether or not we were really working as a couple. I was crushed, but I was determined to handle it maturely. We'd hugged, I'd cried, and even I had to admit that *something* was missing. But what exactly? I didn't know. In retrospect, I suppose you should know someone well before you jump into a relationship, and a guy's box-hauling skills may not be the best indicator of your compatibility. Even if he is cute with a slow-to-curl-up sexy smile. So Rick had suggested we split up for a while. We'd stay friends. Maybe we'd get back together. At that point, I really didn't know. Or maybe I just didn't want to face the truth.

The timing of this decision couldn't have been worse. I'd thought we were going to spend the entire winter break together so I'd told my parents that I was staying on campus. By the time I realized there would be only a handful of students who stayed *and* I'd be without Rick, my parents—planning to tour several southern states—had already packed up their twenty-seven-foot travel trailer and headed for warmer climes.

Yeah, sure, it wasn't too late for me to catch a bus, train, or plane and meet up with them somewhere, but let's get real here. Would you want to spend your winter break constantly within nine yards of your parents?

Me either.

I love them, but the love deepens at a distance.

So I was staying on campus as originally planned. I was just doing it without Rick. I tried to convince myself I didn't care. But who was I trying to kid? It was totally going to suck.

To fill the yawning abyss of time, I'd registered to take two classes during the winter minimester. Two courses crammed into two intense weeks. I was actually kind of looking forward to it, viewed it as a challenge to have to concentrate so intently on the studies. I know. I'm strange. But I didn't have anything better to do and in the long run if I stayed on my graduation plan, I'd finish at least one semester early.

Plus I needed to work and had asked for some extra hours. If I could grab enough shifts, and if the tips from the incoming tourists were as generous as I'd heard they'd be, maybe I could save up for a spring break trip. Do my own version of getting away from it all then. Provided Rick and I didn't get back together.

"Oh, no," Mel said, suddenly taking my arm and turning me toward her. "I know that look. Alyssa, did you guys break up?"

"What? No. Absolutely not." I felt as though I was in a Shakespeare play, protesting too much and hoping she wouldn't notice. Rick and I had agreed not to tell anyone, just in case we got back together. It would be less awkward around our friends that way. No one taking sides while we were apart, trash-talking the other party to show support, and then having to pretend they liked the other person if we became a couple again. "It's just that, well, he went to Australia."

Her hazel eyes widened at that news. If her short red hair wasn't already semi-spiked in a style similar to that of a hissing cat, it might have reacted as well. "Wow! What'd he do? Come into an inheritance?"

I actually laughed. Mel had that effect on me. She made things seem not quite so dire and unmanageable. "No, at least I don't think so. He discovered couch surfing. People let strangers sleep on their couch, and then they go sleep on someone else's couch. Swapping around, I guess."

"*Ew!* Sounds a little too *Hostel* for me. Does he even know these people?"

I'd worried about that too. "He said it was safe. He used an Internet site. People are interviewed or something. I'm not really sure how it all works."

"Still, I think I'd be more comfortable in a five-star hotel."

"Like any of us could ever afford a five-star hotel," I pointed out.

"Not right now, I'll admit, but someday. So how long is Rick gonna be gone?" she asked.

"Until the next semester starts."

"Bummer. I mean, really. Why so long?"

"Wouldn't you want to be there as long as possible? It's not like he can just pop over and pop back. I think it takes, like, a whole day to get there."

"I can't believe how understanding you're being about this," Mel said. "If Boomer headed to another country without me, he could find himself a new girlfriend when he got back."

Boomer had been her boyfriend since high school. Apparently she didn't have relationship issues.

If Rick and I were still totally committed to each other, hadn't decided to take a break from each other, I would have been upset with Rick's leaving me behind. Not that I wanted to sleep on a stranger's couch. And money for an airline ticket was also an obstacle. But we weren't a couple so I had no right to complain. Besides, with Rick gone, I could really concentrate on my studies, right?

Was I expecting too much to want a few fireworks in a relationship?

I supposed that I could talk to Mel, get her opinion on things, but it wasn't as though we'd done any deep soul sharing. We'd bonded over spilled drinks, bitchy customers, and taking up the slack at each other's tables. She, Boomer, Rick, and I had shared a couple of pizzas, sat together at some football games. But we weren't to the point where we could talk about anything and everything.

"That's four weeks of datelessness," Mel continued. "What are you going to do?"

"Take a couple of classes over the minimester. Maybe work some extra hours."

"Omigod! Classes and work over winter break? Are you crazy?"

"You're working," I reminded her.

"Well, yeah, but not extra. You need to spend winter break being wild and carefree!"

"A little late for that."

"You should have discussed this with me earlier. I would have talked you out of it."

"But I want to do it. And with Rick gone, I'm looking at empty hours."

"Okay, but before classes start on Monday, you need to do something totally wild. We'll go to the lodge and have a spa day. Massage, facial, mani-pedi. The works. The tension will melt away. I'll call in the morning and make a reservation."

It sounded heavenly, but the reality was that my budget was stretched a little tight.

"I'm not sure I can afford—"

"I've got a two-for-one couples special coupon."

"Couples? They'll think we're—"

"So? Trust me. I've had a day there before. And no way will Boomer ever again be subjected to what he considers torture."

"He went with you?"

"Well, yeah, because again it was a couples coupon. Anyway, they pamper you like crazy. Even feed you a little lunch with a sparkly brew. When they're finished, you'll be so relaxed, you won't care what they think."

It was so tempting. . . .

"Oh, stop fighting it," she said. "It'll be the best money you ever spent."

My parents *had* sent me some extra money so I could enjoy myself over winter break. I nodded, decision made. "Okay. Let's do it."

"Great! And I'll request a male massage therapist. They have such strong hands."

I think she actually shivered, and I didn't think it was from the cold. We reached the edge of campus where our paths diverged.

"I'll check you later," she said. "And have sweet dreams about Hans with the magic hands."

Laughing, I watched as she hurried down the street toward a house she rented with some other students. As a sophomore she wasn't restricted to living on campus like I was.

Because the town had a low crime rate, so low it was practically nonexistent, I felt comfortable walking on alone, even though it was so late. Besides, I carried pepper spray in my jacket pocket. My dad had given it to me when I left for college.

The wind picked up. Snow was falling more heavily.

As I approached Wilson Hall, I couldn't help but think it looked deserted. It was more of a residential house than a typical dorm. Painted a light blue that reminded me of a winter sky, it was built in a Victorian style, with white decorative trim and a steep roof. It had four floors, and each floor had several suites. Very quaint and cozy.

I turned up the short walkway that led to the front steps. Out of the corner of my eye I saw someone—large and broad—lurch out from the shadows at the side of the house. Startled, I stepped back, blinking rapidly against the fat snowflakes that were hampering my visibility. The only things that registered were that I didn't know him, he was moving fast, and he looked to have the power of a bulldozer. With survival reflexes kicking in, I yanked the pepper spray out of my jacket pocket and I sprayed him in the face before darting past him.

"What the f—" His curses were muffled because he dropped to the ground and face-planted in the snow.

Then I heard, "What'd you do that for?"

The guy sounded completely baffled instead of angry or mean. But more intriguing, he spoke with an Australian accent. I was a sucker for accents and halfway wished he'd said something as he'd been approaching at lightning speed. I might not have been so quick to react. Or maybe I still would have. A stranger near midnight? Coming out of the shadows? What was I supposed to think?

He sure wasn't there to sell Boy Scout popcorn.

I stopped my frantic attempt to slip the keycard into the slot. My hands were shaking so badly that I couldn't get the alignment right anyway. I needed to calm down.

I looked back over my shoulder. The guy had straightened and was kneeling with his snow-filled hands cupped over his eyes. Keeping my finger poised on the pepper spray nozzle, I crept slowly toward the edge of the porch, glancing around quickly to make sure no one else was about to come rushing forward. "Who are you?"

My voice sounded all high and squeaky. Maybe because I was close to hyperventilating.

"Jude. Jude Hawkins." He'd pushed the gravelly words out through clenched teeth. "Dammit! It hurts like the devil."

He sounded as though he was in serious pain. Guilt shot through me. I glanced around again. Still no one else. He was alone, but the question remained . . .

"Why are you here?" I demanded, grateful to sound a little more in control and less like air leaking out of a balloon.

He scooped up more snow, dropped his head back, and put the icepack he'd fashioned out of the mounds over his eyes. "How long is it gonna sting?"

He appeared fairly harmless now, which was the whole point of pepper spray, I guessed. Still I felt badly that I'd reacted first and was asking questions later. It wasn't like me to panic. But then very few people were still on campus—just those of us working, taking mini-mester courses, or hanging around for the snow. I hadn't expected anyone to burst out of the shadows. "I'm not sure. About half an hour or so, maybe longer."

He groaned, and even his groan seemed to have an Australian accent.

"I'm really sorry, but what are you *doing* out here? I mean, it's late and you were lurking in the shadows. . . ."

Snow fell from one side of his face, maybe because he'd raised an eyebrow to give me a heated glare—and had obviously thought better of it, because he reached for more snow.

"I wasn't lurking. I was staying out of the wind and snow, waiting for someone to come along and let me in. The door's locked."

So was he visiting someone?

"Yeah, they're keeping it locked over winter break," I said. With so few students around, they thought it would lessen the chances of vandalism or anyone coming in who shouldn't. Like my mystery guy. "Do you know someone who's living here? Is there someone I should get for you?"

"All I need is the couch."

"The couch?"

"Yeah. A bloke swapped couches with me."

Okay, logic had run off when panic arrived, but it was slowly starting to return. A sneaky suspicion began working its way through my locked-down brain. "Uh, who offered you a couch?"

"Bloke named Rick. Rick Whirly. You know him?"

"Um, yeah." Rick must have offered Jude the couch in his suite in exchange for a couch in Australia. I sank down into the snow. "I am *so* sorry."

With his gloved hands, he brushed the snow off his face and squinted at me. "Are you Alyssa Manning?"

"How did you know?"

"He mentioned you."

I wondered what he'd said. Was it before or after we'd decided we needed a break from each other? At this point, did it really matter?

"Unfortunately he didn't tell me about you," I confessed.

"Huh. That's odd."

Actually, it wasn't. Rick was the strong, silent type found in romance novels. Well, maybe not so strong, but definitely silent. He was as minimalistic with his words as he was with his lifestyle. Part of the reason our relationship was a little disappointing. I wanted communication between us. Rick thought kissing *was* communication. And okay, on some level it was, but I wanted words as well. I wanted to know what he thought and felt.

Reaching out, I wrapped my hand around Jude's arm. "Come on. Let's get you inside so

I can look at the damage. Blink as fast as you can. I read somewhere it helps. Creates a natural wash like eye drops or something." I was babbling as I pulled him up to his feet.

"What *was* that anyway? What'd you spray in my face?" he asked, and his sexy accent made me wish *he* was the one doing the babbling.

"Pepper spray," I reluctantly confessed.

"That's illegal in Australia."

"Yeah, it is in some states here, too." I wasn't sure about Vermont. I guessed I'd discover the legal ramifications if he were to bring charges against me. Maybe I'd be lucky and it wouldn't occur to him to report me and my pepper spray to the authorities.

Jude stumbled.

"Whoa!" I cried, grabbing him and trying to stop his fall.

But he was way bigger than I was. We tumbled sideways off the walk onto the snow-covered ground with a *whump*, Jude sprawled on top of me.

The distant streetlights and moonlight cast a faint glow over us. Jude was blinking, squinting, his face scrunched up. But even all scrunched, he was too cute for words. I was really wishing we'd started this encounter totally differently—like without me coming off as a crazed psycho girl.

"Sorry about that," Jude said.

I felt this odd sort of excitement, like waiting for the first burst of fireworks on New Year's Eve. It was strange. We weren't doing anything and yet anticipation sparked through me. It was weird. I'd never felt this way with Rick.

But the snow was beginning to melt through my black pants. So as much as I hated to end this moment of having a hunk so near, I said, "Uh, you know what? We can get inside more quickly if you get off me."

"Oh, right, sorry. I can barely think through this hideous pain."

"Is it really that bad?" I asked, horrified at the thought. What if I'd sprayed too much? What if I needed to take him to the emergency room?

"Nah, my eyes are just feeling like they're on fire now. Before I thought they'd been nuked." He rolled awkwardly off me, as though he was groping to figure out where he was. "I hope I'm not gonna go blind. Wouldn't that be a jolly good beginning to a holiday?"

"It's not supposed to cause any permanent damage," I said. At least I didn't think it was. Why hadn't I read the instructions more carefully?

Taking hold of his arm again, I led him up the steps and across the porch to the door. I took the keycard out of my jacket pocket and slipped it into the card reader. The door made a clicking noise. I turned the knob and opened it.

Thank goodness no one was downstairs. I really wanted to keep this situation on the down-low. For all eternity, if possible.

I guided the wounded Aussie to the kitchen. The light over the sink was always left on, so people could easily find their way to the kitchen for a late-night snack.

"Here, sit down." I pulled out a chair.

He sat with a thud. "I should have brought in some snow."

"I'm going to get you some milk."

"No, thanks. I don't much like milk. Could use a beer, though." His voice was getting louder with each frustrating minute.

"No beer, sorry. And we kinda need to keep quiet. After ten, only residents and guests approved by the dorm monitor are allowed inside. At this point I'm not sure you're approved."

I poured milk into a bowl, grabbed a dish towel, and took a seat at the table. I dipped the towel into the milk. Jude pulled off his knit cap. He had brown hair that had streaks of blond and reddish gold running through it. It reminded me of the autumn leaves I enjoyed so much. The skin around his eyes was blotchy. Once again guilt prickled through me. "I read somewhere that milk will ease the sting."

He squinted and looked down with disgust. "I really don't think washing my face with milk is the way to go here."

He blinked several times. "They're feeling better, to be honest. I think the blinking helped." He nodded. "Yeah, I think it's gonna be okay."

If not having any white in your eyes was okay. They were seriously bloodshot. If not for the redness, Jude's eyes might have been the most beautiful I'd ever seen. They were an emerald green, deep and velvety looking.

"You're prettier than your picture," Jude said.

I realized he'd been studying me as closely as I was him. I felt the heat rush to my cheeks. "My picture?"

"Yeah, Rick sent me a picture of you. You know. We exchanged photos, tried to bridge the thousands of miles that separated us. He said you're *the one*."

I was stunned. I was *the one*? Then why did Rick suggest we go our separate ways for a while? Was he afraid of what he was feeling? If only we'd discussed what he was feeling! If only he'd told me how important I was to him! "Really? He said I was the one?"

Jude grinned, and a little dimple appeared in one cheek. It was the sexiest grin I'd ever seen. "Absolutely. I can show you."

He tugged off his gloves and put them on the table. He unzipped an outer pocket on his jacket, reached inside, and pulled out a piece of paper. He unfolded it and handed it to me.

It was an email from Rick.

Hello, mate! LOL. I'm practicing my Australian. How am I doing? I'll be crashing on your couch by the time you crash on mine but don't worry. If you run into any problems, just find Alyssa Manning. She'll take care of them, whatever they are. She can show you around, find you some cheap eats, make sure you have a good time. Whatever you need, just ask her. She's super considerate and dependable.

Your couch-swapping mate,
Rick

Oh. Not *the one* in a romantic sense, and I couldn't believe the best compliment he could give me was that I'm considerate. But more shocking was the fact that his letter contained more words than Rick usually spoke to me in an entire day. When his fingers were doing the talking, silent Rick apparently wasn't so silent.

I lifted my gaze to Jude. He was still grinning, as though everything was going to be okay. Problem-solver Alyssa was on the job. I felt as though I needed a superhero costume with a cape and a big *P* on the front or something.

Why had Rick done this? He knew I was planning to take courses. He knew I'd be studying. He knew I didn't have time for distractions.

Thanks, Rick. Thanks a lot. Might have been nice to tell me *you were volunteering me to be a one-person welcoming committee to a hot Aussie!*

Chapter 2

Jude had left his duffel bag outside. I held the front door open while he went to retrieve it.

Splitting up with Rick, cramming for finals, working a busy night at the restaurant, and experiencing an intruder scare—even though it had been a false alarm—was catching up with me. I was suddenly overwhelmed with exhaustion. Once I delivered Jude to Chad—Rick's roommate—I planned to crawl into bed for the duration, or until I needed to get ready for work tomorrow. Or until Mel called with our spa time.

Jude came back in, stomping his feet, rubbing his hands. Earlier, he'd stuffed his gloves into his pockets. Maybe he thought he wouldn't need them for the quick trek outside.

"Gawd! It's cold out there."

I didn't want to discourage him from talking, because I loved the way every word sounded, but I put my finger to my lips. "We need to be quiet, because of that whole unauthorized-people-in-the-dorm-after-ten thing. Something tells me Rick didn't notify the dorm monitor of the arrangement he made with you."

We didn't want to wake up Rules-we-must-live-by Susan, our dorm monitor. She was always slipping reminders into our mailboxes explaining that overnight guests weren't allowed unless she was notified and approved them. And guests of the opposite sex were definitely not allowed in the rooms under any circumstances. *Puh-leeze,* she had more rules than my parents did.

"Oh, right. Yeah. I can see where that might be a problem," Jude whispered.

"Not one that can't be overcome. We just need to . . . not get caught. This way," I said in a low voice, and escorted him to the stairs.

At the second floor, I led him down the hallway to Rick's suite. I knelt down and looked under the door. Lights were still on and I could hear pinging, like the sound effects of a sci-fi movie or a video game. Thank goodness, Chad was still up. I stood, smiled at Jude, and gave him a thumbs-up. He grinned back at me. Everything was going to be just fine. And tomorrow Chad could deal with getting the required approval and any other problems that came up.

I rapped my knuckles on the door and we waited. I heard some scuffling. I gave Jude another smile and knocked again, a little more loudly.

Chad opened the door and the overpowering aroma of a thousand dirty socks wafted into the hallway. It reminded me of the locker room at the gym, only worse.

"Hey, Chad," I said. "This is Jude. I'm sure Rick told you about him."

Chad shook his head. "No."

"He's from Australia?" I prompted, trying to jog his memory.

"Is that a question? You don't know?"

"No, I know he's from Australia. I thought maybe Rick had mentioned him."

Chad smiled. "No, but that's awesome, dude. Rick just headed down there. What are the odds, right?"

Better than you'd think, I thought.

"Uh, actually, that's the reason we're here," I said. "Rick told Jude that he could crash on his couch."

Chad's smile disappeared like snow in summer. "No way, Alyssa. He didn't tell me that."

He said it as though I was the bad guy here, the one responsible for this little snafu.

Then he opened the door a little wider, and I could see guys sprawled on the floor, all with their shoes off. That explained the unusual sock-scented potpourri.

"I've got my brothers and some friends staying over. You know, for the snow. My suitemates invited some guys too. Like, I don't want to be rude, but we're packed in tighter than a toboggan team going down a run."

"Yeah, mate, I can see that," Jude said, before I started to argue that surely they could squeeze in one more guy. Although I did have concerns about the health of anyone exposed to the sock emissions. Maybe Jude had concerns as well. That might explain his gracious acceptance of the situation. "Don't worry about it. I'll figure something out."

"Great, man. I'm really sorry." Chad looked at me, as though again it was my fault that he hadn't known. "But Rick—"

"I'll take care of it," I interrupted. What alternative did I have except to be as gracious as Jude?

"Later, dude." Chad closed the door. I sighed. What now?

"Not to worry," Jude said, as though I'd voiced my concerns out loud. Maybe I had. I was so tired, I could barely think. "I saw a couch downstairs. I can use that. No problem."

How I wished that was true!

"Unfortunately, it's against the rules. But, uh . . . " My roomie, Sheli, had already left. My suitemate, Stephanie, was still here, but she didn't have a roommate. It wasn't as though we would be inconveniencing a lot of people. "You can sleep on the couch in my suite tonight. Maybe in the morning we'll wake up with a better idea."

"Wonderful!"

Where did he get his energy? Then I realized

that in Australia, it was probably daytime.

"This way," I said with more enthusiasm than I felt.

I led us back to the stairs and up to the next floor where I had a corner suite. I slipped my key into the lock, opened the door slightly, reached a hand inside to flip the light switch, and peered inside. Stephanie was not exactly Miss Modesty. Fortunately, she wasn't up, lounging around in her underwear. I moved into the room and closed the door after Jude followed me in.

"Nice flat," he said.

I'd watched enough British movies to know he was referring to an apartment. The living area was really compact with room for only a couch, a small table, and a few floor pillows.

"Thanks. You can sleep on the couch there. I'll grab the comforter off my bed for you."

I went into my bedroom and looked at the empty bed where my roommate would have been sleeping if she hadn't gone home for winter break. I felt a small measure of guilt for not offering it—but I'd known this guy for less than an hour. Sharing the suite I could handle.

Sharing the room was above and beyond.

I dragged the comforter off my bed, bundled it up in my arms, snatched my extra pillow, and went back into the living area.

"Here you go," I said, offering Jude what little I had.

"I really appreciate all this. I thought everything was arranged."

I gave him a reassuring smile. "It'll all work out. Stephanie, my suitemate, is pretty cool, so maybe she'll be okay with you staying here. I'm okay with it."

I was really tired, but it seemed rude to just leave.

"Do you want some chips, something to drink?" I felt like such an inadequate hostess.

"Nah, I ate earlier, but thanks. No need to keep me company. You look like you're about to fall asleep, anyway."

"Yeah, busy night at work." I jerked my thumb over my shoulder. "So, if you're okay—"

"I'm perfectly comfortable."

He was certainly perfect. "All right, then. I'm going on to bed. If you do think of something you need just rap on my door." I took a step back. "So, good night."

"G'night."

I slipped back into the bedroom and closed the door. I pressed my ear against the thin wood, feeling like a spy. I heard the couch moan. I imagined Jude stretching out and knew he wouldn't fit.

Pulling my cell phone out of my pocket, I sat on the edge of my bed. I tried calling Rick and got his voice mail, so I left him a message.

"We need to talk. It's urgent. Call me as soon as you get off the plane."

I closed my phone. There was nothing more I could do tonight.

Apparently the "nothing more" included not sleeping. I was exhausted but it was as though someone had dropped a bucket of Ping-Pong balls in my head and my thoughts were bouncing around crazily.

I kept listening for Jude to make some noise, to be creeping around the suite. Was I insane to trust this guy just because he had an email from Rick? Hadn't I thought Rick was nuts to head halfway around the world to sleep on a stranger's couch? And what had I done? I'd put a stranger on *my* couch in, like, two seconds flat.

A stranger I couldn't stop thinking about. God, he was cute when he said g'night.

I thought I drifted off for a while. But when I rolled over and squinted at the clock on the bedside table, it was barely morning. Still, I wanted to be awake and with Jude when Stephanie woke up. Yeah, she was normally cool, but then these weren't normal circumstances.

I rolled out of bed and shuffled to the bathroom. After a quick shower, I threw on some thick woolen socks, gray sweatpants, and a red sweatshirt—because honestly red was my color. I wanted to look good without looking like I'd gone to any trouble. What was wrong with me? I pulled my long, black hair into a ponytail. I had layered bangs that framed my face and curled around my chin. All the black made my deep blue eyes stand out like gemstones.

With Rick gone, I'd planned to be incredibly low maintenance, but the hot Aussie in the living room was making me rethink that decision. Not that I was going to make a play for a guy who was going to be in my life for just three or four weeks. No, after giving it some thought when I couldn't sleep, I'd decided I was content to play the role of problem solver and tour guide—at least until classes started. After that, we'd see.

I opened the bedroom door and peered into the living room. The only light came from the muted flickering TV. I crept over to the couch.

It looked as if Jude had taken off only his boots and his jacket. The comforter was half on him, half on the floor, leaving his sock-clad feet exposed. He was wearing jeans and a blue sweatshirt with a UQ on it and what looked like a coat of arms. His university maybe? Someplace he'd visited? Was he even a student? How old was he? What did he do other than sleep on people's couches?

I could see him a bit clearer now. His hair—thick and straight, not a curl to be found—was longer than I realized, hanging past his ears. To my immense relief, it appeared that the puffiness from the pepper spray had gone away. I was vampire pale while he was sun bronzed. He was Hugh Jackman hot.

Jude's eyes fluttered open, and he gave me the grin that already seemed incredibly familiar. "G'day."

I released a tiny giggle and clapped my hand over my mouth to stifle the embarrassing sound. Who giggled just because she was greeted? But his voice had sounded so cute.

His grin grew as he pulled his legs back and sat up. "What?"

"That greeting seems, so, I don't know. Australian."

"I s'pose because it is." He stretched, raising his arms over his head and groaning as though every muscle and bone ached. He scooted over to make room on the couch for me to sit. I plopped down into the corner, keeping some distance between us. I was completely intrigued by his relaxed pose, his easygoing manner. It invited friendship.

"So do you do this a lot? Traveling, sleeping on couches?" I asked.

"I did it last summer, going through Britain, so thought I'd give the U.S. a try."

"And you decided Vermont was the place to start?"

"To be honest, I wasn't sure where I wanted to go, not until I met Rick on-line. He told me about the snow, the mountains. He made it all sound like a winter wonderland. I'm not used to weather such as you've got here, so I thought why not? Have a go at it. If I don't like it, I can always move on."

I couldn't imagine such an unstructured existence.

"So how long were you thinking of staying here?"

"I've got a month before I have to get back. So far, from the little bit I've seen, I've got to say that the snow is amazing."

"You say that as though you've never seen snow."

"I've seen it but not this much. Doesn't snow in the part of Australia where I live. We're more balmy and coastal. You know, sand and surf."

That explained his tan.

"Gets a bit chilly in the winter, but nothing like this," he continued.

How could it be winter without snow? I

appreciated every season, but winter was my favorite. I loved when it was time to pull out my thick sweaters. I loved the smell of a wood fire. I loved skiing and snowboarding and sledding, when I could find the time—although time was in short supply when school was in session. I even enjoyed the cold, wintry weather. It was great for snuggling.

"I've been in Vermont forever," I said. "I can't imagine not living in weather like this."

"I've been in Australia all my life. So there you are. It's great if you love the water, which I do. But I was in the mood to try something different. Rick thought this would be it."

I couldn't even begin to imagine the astounding number of words it would have taken for Rick to convince him of that. The guy I'd believed couldn't communicate apparently could when he set his mind to it. Interesting. I was learning more about Rick in the short time I'd known Jude than I had in the four months I'd known Rick.

"Did you ring Rick up last night?" Jude suddenly asked.

"*Ring* him?"

With his hand, he made the universal signal for phone.

"Oh, call him. No. Well, yes. I called, but we didn't connect. I left him a message. Not sure what he can really tell us, though. Not unless there's a hidden couch somewhere."

Jude furrowed his brow. "That's probably not likely, is it?"

I nodded grimly. "No, probably not, which means he probably won't be much help."

Jude studied me for a minute. "So what are the plans?"

"Well, barring a secret couch, I'll talk with Stephanie. Like I said last night, she might be okay with you staying here. One slight problem. Guys aren't allowed on this floor after midnight, so we'd have to sneak you around."

"I'm good at sneaking."

Considering our encounter last night, that went without saying.

The door to the other bedroom opened and Stephanie—she was always Stephanie, never Steph—stepped out wearing flannel pajamas. She had curly brown hair, and first thing in the morning, it usually looked as though she'd stuck her finger in a socket. Her brown eyes were opened wide.

She arched a brow at me. "Uh, *hello*?! What's going on here?"

Chapter 3

Jude had her at g'day.

"I love an Aussie accent," she said. "Say something else."

Jude laughed. It was the first time I'd heard him laugh, and I swear, it too rang with an accent. "Now, you've put me on the spot."

Stephanie giggled lightly and repeated *spot*, saying it the way he had, somehow hiding the vowel. A lot of his words sounded shorter than they actually were.

"How cute is that? Totally," Stephanie said.

Stephanie was in the habit of often asking a question and answering it herself. I wasn't quite sure if she was mental and carrying on conversations with herself or if she didn't have the patience to wait for the answers.

"You are the absolute cutest," she went on.

Then she shifted her gaze to me and crooked her finger. "Uh, can I see you in private for a minute?"

"If you don't mind, I'm going to pop into the loo," Jude said, pointing toward my bedroom.

"Uh, yeah sure. Actually"—I got up—"hold on just a sec."

I hurried into my room. *Who's mental now, Alyssa?* I asked myself as I dashed madly around picking up discarded clothes. I tended to avoid hangers when I didn't have a roommate around who might object to tripping over clothes. Sheli had finished finals early and left a few days ago, so I'd immediately thrown caution to the wind. My clothes had suffered as a result.

Then I ducked into my bathroom to make sure I hadn't left any underwear or personal items lying around. Why hadn't it occurred to me that eventually he was going to need access to a bathroom?

Okay, okay, okay. I straightened things, placed a couple of clean towels on the counter, and calmly walked back into the living room. Hanging on to Jude's every word, Stephanie was sitting on the edge of the coffee table. What did I care if she was ogling him and he was interested in her? Not my business. But I still had this strange urge to break up their conversation.

"It's ready," I said.

"I'll visit with you more in a bit, Stephanie." Jude stood up and grabbed his duffel bag. He winked as he walked by me. I wasn't sure why or what it meant but it made me feel special.

Stephanie's eyes followed him as he disappeared into my bedroom and closed the door.

"Omigod! Is he not the cutest?" Stephanie asked. "Where did you find him?"

"In the front yard," I said truthfully, surprised he hadn't shared every sordid detail. Then I told her all about last night's misadventures. When I finished, she said, "So Rick made these arrangements and didn't tell anyone?"

"Apparently. So how do you feel about letting Jude stay here?"

"As long as he's using your *loo* and not mine. But if we get caught, it's your problem."

I felt an amazing sense of relief. I really

hadn't wanted to let Jude down. "I think I can handle that."

By the time Jude came out of my bedroom, Stephanie had left to spend the day on the slopes with some friends.

I put my hand beneath my chin, striving for nonchalance as I worked to keep my jaw from dropping.

Omigod! Freshly showered, Jude looked absolutely amazing. He was wearing a forest green cable-knit sweater which really brought out the deep green of his gorgeous eyes. Now that they no longer contained a hint of red, they were even more beautiful. If his emerging from my room hadn't knocked the breath out of me, noticing his eyes would have.

I suddenly felt very awkward. I didn't know what to do with my hands, because they wanted to reach out and brush his autumn-colored hair off his brow. I tucked them beneath my arms, as though they were cold. Actually nothing about me was cold. Jude somehow had the ability to raise my temperature to the point that I probably appeared fevered.

"So what's the verdict?" he asked.

"Stephanie is okay with you staying in our suite. So our couch is yours if you want it."

"Do you have a problem with it?" he asked.

"What? No, not at all." Did I sound too eager? I thought I sort of did. He was fascinating, and what I'd thought was going to be an uneventful winter break suddenly had possibilities.

Jude gave me a big grin. "Fantastic."

"So what are your plans for the day?" I asked.

"Take a walkabout. Want to come with me?"

"You know, I would but I need to go to the campus bookstore."

"I like bookstores."

That was all I really needed to do today. Pick up my books for Monday's classes. So why not?

We walked to a little pancake house near campus. I'd changed into jeans and a curve-hugging red sweater. I'd felt a compulsion to at least look like someone Jude wouldn't be embarrassed to be seen with—although he seemed to just go with the flow, no matter how turbulent it might be.

He ordered scrambled eggs, crisp bacon, sausage, biscuits, and a "cuppa tea." I ordered buttermilk pancakes and a glass of skim milk.

It was a bright clear day. The snow that had come through the night before had left a fresh blanket of white, but most of the sidewalks and the roads were already cleared. When you live in snow country, the city is always prepared.

"So how'd you get into couch swapping?" I asked, pouring maple syrup over my pancakes.

"Money."

"There's money to be made in it?"

He crumbled his bacon over his eggs, stirred them up. "No, my lack of money. You read the note, right? Rick said you'd hook me up with some cheap eats."

Considering how much Jude was eating for breakfast, I didn't think I'd have much luck in that department. Maybe it was my fascination with watching *$40 a Day with Rachael Ray* that had convinced Rick I was the cheap-eats go-to girl. She could go to any city and eat all day without spending more than forty dollars. She always had interesting meals—and everything was absolutely delicious. Just once, I wanted to see her taste something, grimace, and say, "Okay, this was a bad choice."

But I didn't want Jude to know that I had concerns about delivering on the inexpensive food. It would be a challenge, but not impossible.

"Speaking of eats, you absolutely can't come to Vermont and not have our maple syrup." I nudged my plate nearer to him. "Help yourself."

He grinned. "You're such a small thing, you should finish them."

I'd never had anyone refer to me as small. I was short and relatively slender, but I held my own when it came to scarfing down food. "I'm not offering you the whole plate. Just a few bites." I pushed the syrup toward him. "Pour some more on so you get the full flavor."

I watched as he drenched a portion of the pancakes in syrup. Using a fork and knife—I didn't know anyone who used a knife on pancakes—he sliced neatly through the stack, created perfect little wedges, and gathered up the pieces with the fork. He popped them into his mouth. His eyes got really wide as he chewed. "Now, that's smashing."

"We're famous for our maple syrup. My dad pours maple syrup on everything."

"Can't say I blame him. What's your dad do?"

"He actually just unscrews the top, removes it, and pours syrup like there's no tomorrow. He can't stand the tops with the little holes. Says they're as slow as tapping a maple tree."

Jude laughed, and again I was struck by what a wondrous sound it was. "No. I meant what's he do for a living."

"Oh yeah, of course." I wanted to crawl beneath the table. What made me think he'd care how my dad poured syrup? My thoughts this morning were obviously as scrambled as the eggs Jude had eaten. "Uh, he's in real estate. My mom, too. Family business. Struggling family business at the moment, but as my mom is fond of saying, 'what goes down must come up.' Although I'm not sure that's exactly true, because that scenario sort of defies gravity."

He grinned at my babbling. Even when I

was talking nonsense he paid attention. I wondered if he found my New England accent fascinating.

"Is that what you're gonna do?" he asked. "Go into the family business?"

"No. I want to go to med school. Be a pediatrician."

"Take care of ankle biters?"

I gave him an exaggerated, teasing grimace. "Come on! Kids aren't that bad."

"They're little buggers. I have three brothers, all much younger. They're a pain in my bum. And I have a sister, a tad older, who I think is pretty cool. What about you?"

"Are you asking if I'm a pain in your bum?"

He laughed. "You're not. Absolutely not. I was asking if you have any brothers or sisters."

"Nope, it's just me." Using my fork, I cut off some pancake. "So is it weird? Sleeping on strangers' couches?"

"Not so far. I like it, actually. Gives me a chance to get to know the people and the customs of wherever I'm visiting. Like this, for example." Using his knife, he pointed toward the pancakes. "If I was on my own, I might have never tried the maple syrup. Which is marvelous, by the way. But I'd have never known if you hadn't shared."

"Didn't you research Vermont before heading over here? Didn't you know we have world-famous syrup?"

"Not really." He grinned. "I like being surprised, learning as I go. Coming here with no preconceived notions of what to expect. Well, except for the snow and the cold, of course. Makes every day an adventure."

I shook my head. "See, I like to have everything planned out."

"Nothing wrong with that. But I'm thinking my spontaneous way is a bit more fun; leaves opportunities for unexpected possibilities."

I wasn't sure it was *his way* as much as it was *him*. He struck me as someone who really brought the party with him.

"Isn't it lonely, traveling alone?"

"Nah, I've got you, now haven't I?"

I felt this silly tightening in my chest. What he said might have been the sweetest thing anyone ever said to me.

"Besides, if I was traveling with someone," Jude continued, "I'd probably spend all my time visiting with my mate and talking to him, instead of talking to the strangers around me. I wouldn't learn a lot about the people in the country I'm visiting. What's the point in that? Traveling and not getting to know the people?"

"I never thought of it like that."

"I like sightseeing, don't get me wrong. I like seeing the buildings and the monuments and the museums, but the people fascinate me. And you never know who you're going to meet." He shifted in his seat and I could see the excitement rippling off of him. "Last year, I'm riding the tube in London—that's the underground railway by the way—and I'm talking to this bloke. Turns out he works for Scotland Yard. He took me on a private tour of the place. Fascinating."

I didn't think it could have been nearly as fascinating as Jude.

"So I enjoy meeting people. I can see my mates when I'm home. But the world, I just want to explore it."

When we finished eating, we bundled back

up and headed outside. The day was clear. The air was crisp, but cold enough to create an ache in my lungs.

I took Jude on the grand tour of the campus, trying to remember some of the things I'd been told about its history during orientation.

"You don't have to be my official tour guide," he finally said.

I blushed, realizing I might be taking my role too seriously. I was spouting off facts and figures that I didn't think anyone really cared about.

"I'm not too good at it," I confessed. "Trying to make history and facts interesting. I don't have a flair when it comes to being a storyteller. I can point out the building where I had classes with a certain degree of authority."

"I just like to look around," he assured me.

As traditional as the campus was, with its redbrick buildings, it also possessed an intimacy that I'd always liked. Glancing over at Jude, seeing how relaxed his facial features were, I was fairly certain that he noticed the welcoming feel of the campus.

"How's your face today?" I asked.

He shifted his eyes over to me. "Not bad. Stings a bit but nothing to worry over."

"I'm not sure I would have been as understanding if someone had attacked me with pepper spray."

"It was sorta Rick's fault, now wasn't it?"

I nodded. Rick was at the bottom of the whole mess, although I was starting to view it as less of a mess and as more of an interesting development. I'd never met or visited with anyone from Australia. As a matter of fact, I couldn't remember ever talking with anyone who wasn't American.

"So I've got no hard feelings," Jude continued, "but you can make it up to me."

"Oh?"

"Yeah."

He unzipped his jacket pocket and took out a tiny digital camera. "If I take some photos, will you let me upload them on your computer and send them home?"

"Oh, sure, not a problem."

"Fantastic." He held up the camera and clicked a picture of me.

"Oh, no!" I covered my face. "I hate candids!"

He laughed. "Why?"

I looked at him through splayed fingers. "My nose was red. My mouth was probably in some absurd shape."

"You looked great. 'Sides, I don't like the posed pics. They're not the real person. They're a reflection of what the person wants the world to think of her—not what she really is."

I'd never thought of it that way. "But if that's the image she wants to leave behind, shouldn't you respect that?"

"How's this? I'll take pictures my way, and any you don't like, I'll delete—no arguments."

Why did he want pictures of me anyway? To serve as a reminder of the unprepared tour guide/problem solver who'd been responsible for the most boring vacation of his life?

"Deal," I said, deciding it didn't really matter. I wanted him to have a picture of me. And maybe I could sneak in a shot or two of him.

"Did you want me to take a picture of you?" I asked.

"Nah. My mates know what I look like." He

snapped a picture of a building.

"So what does UQ stand for?" I asked, thinking of the sweatshirt he was wearing last night.

"University of Queensland."

"Is that where you go to school?"

"Yeah. Studying aeronautical engineering."

"Ah, then you're a genius."

"Nah. Just study a lot. That's the reason I take these trips. Get away from it all for a bit. Revitalize myself."

"I was thinking about doing that over spring break. Just ditching the whole academic world for a few days."

"You could come to the Land of Oz."

I laughed, envisioning me arriving on a twister. "The Land of Oz?"

"That's what we call Australia."

"Thought you called it the Land Down Under."

"That, too. I mean, you don't just call Vermont *Vermont*, do ya?"

"No, we're also the Green Mountain State."

"See, that's too long for us. We shorten things. If we give something another name, it's usually shorter than the original. Like barbecue is barbie. Crocodile is croc. Alyssa is Lys."

He said it all so naturally. "I've never had anyone call me anything except Alyssa."

"Do you mind me calling you just Lys?"

"Just Lys?" I pretended to think about it. "So if you wanted my attention, you'd shout, 'Hey! Just Lys!'"

"Ah, funny. Maybe I *will* call you Just Lys. Serves you right for being difficult."

I gave him an impish smile. "Lys is fine. Actually, I like Lys." Of course, he could call me dirt with that lovely accent of his and I'd like it. I was pathetic.

"I like her too."

"No." Now I was laughing. "No, I meant the name. How can we have a communication problem when we both speak the same language?"

"Well, it's not quite the same, now is it?"

"You're right. I like the way you talk much better."

And the way he grinned and the way he laughed and the way he looked when he was sleeping . . . and when he wasn't sleeping.

"You know," he began, "I have a list of a

hundred things to do before I die—"

"Omigod!" My chest felt like it was caving in on itself as I gasped. "You're terminally ill."

"What? No! I'm not dying. I mean, not anytime soon anyway. Gawd, you're a pessimist."

"I'm sorry. I thought you were talking about a bucket list—like that movie with Morgan Freeman and Jack Nicholson."

"No. No. There are just things I want to do in life, so I keep a list so I don't forget. Anyway, I was going to say before you panicked—"

"I didn't panic."

"You panicked. Made me feel good, actually, that you'd care. But anyway. On my list is to build a snowman. So where does a bloke go around here to learn how to do that?" he asked, wearing that now familiar grin.

"I don't like to brag," I said, "but I am somewhat of an expert when it comes to building snowmen."

Chapter 4

"So a snowball really does collect more snow as it rolls along," Jude said, amazement in his voice.

I'd brought him to a nearby park and was demonstrating how to create the first of three balls that would make up the snowman. A few people were out with their dogs but other than that it was pretty deserted today.

"Well, yeah. What'd you think?"

"I thought it was just something that happened in cartoons. You know, like someone jumping on a trampoline and flying into outer space. Doesn't happen in real life."

"Okay, I missed that one about jumping on a trampoline. But yeah, snow is not to be messed with."

He began packing some snow together for

the next ball before I'd finished the first.

"I probably have a pen in my backpack that we can use for the nose. Plus I'm always dropping peppermint starlights into my pack so I'll sacrifice those for the eyes. If you don't mind it having red eyes."

"Then she'll look like me from last night."

"She?"

"Yeah. I thought I'd make a snowwoman."

I turned toward him. "This is a public—"

Splat!

A snowball hit my shoulder. I very slowly dusted it off my coat, then gave Jude a hard stare. He was grinning like he was about six years old.

"I've always wanted to do that," he said.

"You might want to rethink your strategy, Aussie, because I have a lot more snowball fights—"

Splat!

That one hit me right in the chest, leaving "under my belt" unsaid. Jude started dancing around like he was Rocky preparing for a comeback.

"Let's see what you got!" he taunted. "Let's

see what you got!"

"Okay." I growled low, barely moving my mouth, carefully eyeing him. I would not feel guilty for using my superior snowball fighting skills against him. I packed up a snowball, took careful aim, and flung it.

He easily sidestepped it and laughed. "Is that the best you've got?"

He bent down preparing to take another shot. I quickly moved around behind the ball I'd been rolling and knelt down. I frantically started stocking my arsenal, knowing I wouldn't have much time, knowing he would probably only prepare one snowball.

I heard crunching snow, but didn't stop.

"You can't hide from me," Jude said.

I looked up and took one in the face, one in the shoulder. Clever guy had prepared one for each hand, but that was no match for my handy little soldiers.

He cackled. I scooped one of the snowballs and flung it into *his* face.

"Hey!"

The next one hit his shoulder.

"Here now."

I gathered up three and lobbed them in rapid-fire action, one right after the other. He threw up his hands and staggered back. *Beginner mistake.*

"I tried to warn you!" I yelled, showing him no mercy, giving him no time to regroup.

He was stumbling one way, then the other, trying to scoop up snow. He just flung it at me. A handful of snow. What good was that?

"It's futile to resist!" I yelled, going after him and pelting him with three more carefully aimed snowballs. "Face plant in the snow and surrender!"

Laughing, he tumbled onto his butt.

"That's not a face plant."

He jumped back up. "I wasn't surrendering."

He scrambled toward the jungle gym, fell down, struggled back up, and finally made it to cover, crouching behind the slide. I was scooping and packing snow as I went, cradling the balls in the crook of my arm, held against my chest.

I leaped around the slide, fired away. He lobbed his measly attempt at a snowball at me and raced out from cover. I followed.

When we were clear of the slide, he spun around, lowered his shoulder, and charged.

I screamed and—like a novice—dropped my snowballs and ran.

He tackled me and we both went down, laughing.

"It's futile to resist," he said in a low voice near my ear. "Where did that come from? Darth Vader?"

Breathing heavily, I turned my head, pressing my cheek to the snow. "I think so."

"You have mad snowball fighting skills."

"I tried to warn you."

"Still, I won."

"No way! You cheated."

"What? There are rules in a snowball fight?"

"Absolutely."

"There are no rules in love or war."

He rolled off me, stood up, then extended his hand. I sat up, took it with a two-handed grip, and yanked. He lost his balance and fell face first. I was straddling his back before he knew what hit him.

"Admit it. I won," I demanded.

"Are you competitive or what?"

"I am competitive. I have a four-point-oh G.P.A."

He tried to buck me off, but I clung to him. Gave no quarter.

Laughing, panting, he gasped. "All right. You won."

I bounced off him, stood up, and did a couple of quick victory jumps.

He rolled over and extended his hand. "Help me up."

I folded my arms across my chest and studied him.

"Oh, all right." He pushed himself to his feet. "I'll bet I can build a better sand castle than you."

I nodded graciously. "Yes, you probably can."

He pointed to the one remaining large ball. "Let's get back to that, shall we?"

"Sure." I extended my arm. "After you."

"Nah. I learned my lesson. I will not engage you in another snowball fight. It was fun though. Can't do that with sand."

We started trudging across the park, back to where we'd been.

"So," he said. "A pencil for her nose, candy for her eyes. What about her mouth?"

"Did I not say I was somewhat of an expert at building snowmen?"

"You did."

"Then leave it to me."

Holding plastic cups of hot chocolate, we sat on the back of a metal bench, our feet on the seat, studying our creation. I was in the bad habit of just dropping my change into my backpack and we'd found enough pennies to give our lady a smile. She actually turned out looking pretty good, especially with my neck scarf draped around her. Jude had given her a modest shape, not too risqué for an area where children came to play.

"You know what she needs?" Jude asked.

"Some heels?"

He laughed. "No, a dog."

I swiveled my head around to study him. "A dog?"

Nodding, he took a sip of his hot chocolate.

A little shop was nearby. Everyone stopped there coming to or going from the park. They did quite a brisk little business.

"I've never heard of a snow dog," I confessed. "I guess if we made it sitting or laying down . . ." I couldn't quite picture it.

"I was thinking a poodle. 'Cause they've got all those little furry pom-pom-looking things on them."

"I still think it needs to be sitting. You need all the weight on the bottom."

"All right. Let me think about that for a minute, see if I can get it in my mind."

I couldn't believe how seriously he was taking this project.

"Do you have a dog?" I asked.

"A blue heeler."

I shook my head. "I'm not familiar with that breed."

"Also known as an Australian cattle dog."

"Do you have cattle?"

"No. Just the dog."

"What's his name?"

"Thunder. Don't ask me where I got the

name. I just looked at him and thought, 'His name is Thunder.' So there you are. He stays with my parents when I'm in school. But he's my best mate when I'm at home. What about you? Have any dogs?"

"No, never have had a dog."

"Don't you like them?"

"I do, just never invested in one."

"Everyone should have a dog. Well, actually, no they shouldn't. Only people who love dogs should have dogs." He leaned forward, put his elbows on his thighs. "I did volunteer work with animal rescue for a while. Damn depressing job. And now I've gotten all morbid, haven't I?" He leaped off the bench and tossed his empty cup in the trash can. "I'm going to give her a dog."

I climbed down. "I'll help."

It was late afternoon when we returned to the suite, exhausted. Jude landed on the couch in a reclining position, swearing he wasn't ever going to move again. It had taken us a bit longer than we'd expected to make the snow dog. We had a lot of trial and error, and I'm not sure it was an identifiable breed, but when we were finished, it was cute.

Jude had handed his camera over to someone who was out walking his real dog and the man took a picture of us with our snow creations. Apparently sometimes Jude did break his rule about posed shots.

Then we'd gone to the bookstore to get my books for class. Jude had been appalled to learn I was taking classes over winter break.

"Shouldn't you be relaxing, having fun, preparing for the grind of next semester?"

Had I known he was on the way to my couch, I might not have registered, but I was committed now.

He'd even carried my books. I didn't know guys did that anymore.

After our trip to the bookstore, we'd gone for greasy hamburgers and fries, my treat to make up for the pepper spray incident and because I'd discovered he didn't have anywhere close to forty dollars to spend on food a day. So the Rachael Ray plan was definitely out.

I was going to have to do some serious creative thinking.

I left Jude in his crashed position, while I got ready for work. I took a quick shower and applied a light layer of makeup. I pulled on my black slacks, slipped on my crisply pressed white shirt, and had just finished clipping on my black tie, when Rick called.

"I got your message. I thought we'd agreed to take a break from each other."

"Well, hello to you, too."

I heard him sigh. "Sorry. I wasn't expecting to hear from you, wasn't planning to call you. Are you expecting me to call you? Do I need to do that?" I couldn't believe how defensive he was.

"No, no, we are taking a break. You don't owe me any phone calls. It's just that something came up. Jude?"

"Oh, yeah." His voice perked up with excitement. "Did he get there okay?"

"He got here, but I'm not sure about the okay part. You sorta forgot to tell anyone he was coming," I said.

"What are you talking about? I told you."

"Noooo. Actually you didn't."

"Are you sure?"

I couldn't contain my frustrated sigh. "Yeah, I'm sure. You didn't even tell Chad, and he made his own plans for your couch. And your suite is wall-to-wall guys."

"Oh, man, that's not good. I promised Jude a couch."

So he *wasn't* going to reveal a hidden couch somewhere.

"It doesn't really matter now. When I couldn't get in touch with you last night, I took care of things. Stephanie's okay with him staying on the couch in our suite, so he's bunking there," I told him.

"He's sleeping *where*?"

Hmm, was that jealousy I detected in his voice? Maybe he did miss me after all.

"On my couch. But only because there was nowhere else for him to go." *Thanks to you,* I refrained from adding.

"Well, as long as he has somewhere to stay. I don't want his sister to kick me off her couch."

"Whose sister? Jude's sister? You're staying with Jude's sister?"

He didn't respond. Not even a peep. I pulled my phone away from my ear and looked at it. We'd lost our connection.

I had a feeling more than our phones were no longer connected.

Chapter 5

When I stepped out of my room, to my surprise, Jude was no longer lying on the couch in semiconscious mode. Already sitting up, he looked over his shoulder and grinned. "Ah, there you are. I was about to organize a search party."

He clicked the remote to turn off the TV and got up. "Don't you look formal."

I realized he hadn't gotten a good look at what I was wearing the night before, because I'd kept my parka on.

I made a little *ta-da!* move. "My official work attire. Or as I prefer to call it, my antifeminine costume."

He grinned. "I dunno. You still look pretty feminine to me."

I felt the heat rush to my face. Had I been

fishing for a compliment? Why had I said that? Yes, I'd been slightly offended when Paul, the restaurant manager, gave us all a unisex look, because I'd thought tips would be better if I dressed a little sexier. But the outfit was actually great for working in because I didn't have to wear heels.

I pointed my thumb over my shoulder. "I've got to go. Hopefully Stephanie will be back soon and you'll have some company for the evening." Darkness was settling in so they'd probably already left the slopes.

"I'd rather go with you," Jude said.

"I won't be off work until around eleven."

"Where do you work?"

"A fancy restaurant. The Chalet."

"They've got tables, right?"

"And very expensive menu items."

"How expensive?"

"Veggies would run you at least ten."

"No, they wouldn't. I don't eat veggies."

I smiled. I should have known he wouldn't be deterred. His stubbornness was adorable. "You're looking at forty dollars. At least."

He grimaced. "I see what you mean. All

right, then. I'll walk you to work, then I'll do another walkabout on my own until it's time for you to get off, so I can walk you back to your flat."

"That'll be incredibly boring, waiting for me to get off work—"

"Look, I didn't travel all this way to spend my time staring at four walls or watching the box."

"The box," I'd learned, was his term for TV. I also didn't think he'd come all this way to hang around with me, although I was certainly flattered that he seemed to want to. I nodded, feeling like an incredibly inept tour guide. "Okay."

He rubbed his hands together like he'd just discovered the best thing in the world. "Terrific!"

"I just remembered something—I need to make a quick phone call. I'll be right back." I went to my room. When I returned, Jude was in his jacket, ready to go.

"Now, remember, if we run into anyone, you're staying with Chad," I reminded him.

"Right-o." He walked over to me and wiggled his eyebrows. "Although being able to say

I stayed with you will make for a much better story when I get home."

"Are you ever serious?"

"Not too often. Don't see the point really."

Our good luck continued, and we didn't run into anyone on our way outside. I figured anyone who hadn't gone home for winter break was on the slopes.

It was growing darker as we began walking along the sidewalk, our gloved hands stuffed into our jacket pockets, our breaths turning visible in the frigid air. Jude was hunched a little, probably because he wasn't accustomed to this colder weather. I bundled up, but I never felt really cold. To me, it was invigorating.

"This is so great," Jude said. "All this snow is just spectacular."

"Do you ski?" I asked.

"Nope. And that's a problem, isn't it? You'll have to teach me, right?"

He had a knit cap pulled over his ears, his hair hanging down below it. His cheeks were ruddy. Even in the dimming light, I could see his green eyes sparkling.

"I have to admit I'm not quite the expert at

skiing that I am at building snowmen."

"So? That'll make it more entertaining, right?"

"Could also make it more dangerous. I would hate for you to go home with a broken leg or something."

"Life is all about taking chances."

After a few minutes of silently walking, I ventured to say, "So tell me about your sister."

"Marla? Not much to tell. She's a beaut."

"Rick is staying on her couch?"

"Well, yeah, 'cause I live in a dorm. The room is a tiny box, no couch, and my roommate was going to hang around because of his job. I hate to say it, but he's an ass. I wouldn't inflict him on my worst enemy."

I fought not to smile. Even when he was trash-talking someone he somehow made it entertaining.

"So it wouldn't work for Rick to stay there, but Marla's got a flat nearby. And she's all about couch surfing. She's the one who told me about it."

"And Rick was okay with that? Staying

with Marla, I mean."

"Seemed to be." Studying me, he tilted his head sideways as though the angle would give him a better view. "But you're not."

I shrugged as much as I was able in my jacket. "I don't know. I . . . I just . . . Did he ever tell you that I was his girlfriend?"

Jude came to an abrupt halt. His stunned expression was answer enough. "You're his girlfriend?"

Tears stung my eyes. I hadn't expected that. I wasn't really jealous of Rick staying with Marla. Well, not *too* jealous, anyway. I was just surprised by it. I guess a part of me had wanted him to *want* to stay here over winter break.

"Lys?" Jude's voice was tender, which should have helped, but all it did was make me want to cry more.

"He *was* my boyfriend," I admitted. "But we decided to separate for a while. Take things easy, remain friends. I'm having a hard time defining what we are, because it just sorta came out of the blue right before he left. And it's just left me confused."

"Do you want to get back together?" he asked.

"I don't know. I thought maybe, but"—I shook my head—"I don't know. Rick was my first boyfriend. I guess I haven't really dealt with our decision. God, I haven't even told anyone."

"Why not?"

"Hello? Failure city."

"You're not a failure. Sometimes relationships just don't work out. It's nobody's fault."

He sounded so reasonable. It was the same argument Rick had used with me. I needed to process. But right now I didn't have time.

"I really need to get to work."

I picked up my pace. Jude fell into step beside me.

"You should talk about it," he said.

"I know. And I will." I glanced over at him. "Don't worry. I won't lay it all on you."

"I don't mind. Maybe on the walk home—"

"You came here to have fun, not to listen to my breakup woes."

"As hard as breaking up is, it's better than staying together if things aren't working."

"Are you talking from experience?"

"Maybe." He grinned. "Can't share with you if you won't share with me."

It was amazing. Just a few words from him and I felt better already.

"All right. Maybe later," I said hesitantly.

"As long as I have use of your couch, I'll be around."

When we arrived at The Chalet, Jude gave a little whistle. "Nice. I can see why those veggies are so expensive."

The restaurant was designed to resemble something you'd find in the Swiss Alps. Evergreens had been strategically placed so there was no view of other buildings that might be in the area.

"So I should come back when? Around eleven?" Jude asked.

I grabbed his arm. "First, come around to the back. I have a surprise for you."

"What kind of surprise?"

I was practically giddy at the thought of finally sharing the news. I wasn't usually good at keeping surprises, but I'd wanted to wait until the right moment to spring this one. "A free meal."

His eyes widened. "How'd you manage that?"

"The quick phone call I made before we left? It was to my boss. The employees always get a complimentary meal before we open, and he okayed one for you tonight." I'd gone to my room because I hadn't wanted Jude to hear the call, just in case Paul had said no.

"You're amazing."

The sparkle in his eyes when he looked at me made me feel *amazing,* and my earlier confusing feelings about Rick melted away.

"Come on." I took him around to the back. We went through the door into the kitchen.

Chaos abounded inside. While we set up for the night, the chef would prepare our meals. He wasn't haughty, but he did insist we call him Chef. Our restaurant was the kind that hired chefs, not cooks.

I led Jude to the back office where Paul worked. The door was open. Still I knocked.

Paul looked up from whatever he'd been studying, probably next week's schedule. I smiled at him. He had a face weathered by the cold, winds, ice, and snow. He was a volunteer mountain rescuer. Legend had it he'd climbed Mount Everest. I couldn't imagine how awesome it would be to stand at the top of the world and look down.

I made introductions.

"Sorry, I'm too busy at the moment for chit-chat. Alyssa, give Jude a menu and have him select his dinner with our compliments."

"Thank you, sir," Jude said. "I really appreciate it."

Paul nodded and went back to his papers.

I escorted Jude to the dining room. The lights were turned low. Soft music played in the background. I caught sight of Mel lighting the candle on a nearby table.

"Hey, Mel," I said.

Without turning to look at me, she growled. "Two of the busboys called in sick. Can you believe it?"

Sick? I thought. *Yeah, right*. The first Saturday after finals? Did they think we'd all been born yesterday? Tonight would be more insane than usual.

"Listen, I have someone I want you to meet."

She spun around, looking flustered and PO'd. Then she looked astonished and smiled at Jude. "Oh, hey."

"Mel, this is Jude. Jude, this is Mel Gibson."

Jude released a burst of laughter, then apologized. "Sorry."

"Hey, I get it all the time," Mel said. "My parents have a warped sense of humor. They named me Melinda but they had to know people would call me Mel, so what can you do?"

"Now I'm going to go back home with all kinds of great stories. No one's gonna believe I've met Mel Gibson, but in fact, I have."

She pointed her finger at him. "You're an Aussie." She looked at me speculatively, eyebrow raised.

"It's a long story. I'll explain later. Right now I need to get Jude situated."

I sat him at one of our larger tables, one that most of us usually sat at while we ate. I grabbed a menu and handed it to him. "Look it over. I'll be right back."

I returned to the kitchen, removed my jacket, and hung it on the coat rack near the door. I fished my apron out of my pocket and had barely finished tying it in place when Mel grabbed my arm and spun me around.

"Okay, give me the short version of the long story," she demanded.

"The couch Rick is sleeping on? It isn't exactly free, as it turns out. He swapped his here for that one there, and in typical Rick fashion forgot to tell anyone, except Jude. So I'm playing tour guide."

I almost laughed at the astonished expression on Mel's face. "He's one hot Aussie. So what are you going to do with him?"

"What do you mean?"

She made a little snorting noise. "I think he thinks he has a chance with you."

"No."

"Yes. He doesn't take his eyes off of you."

What was she talking about?

"Of course he does." He'd run into things otherwise. "I need to get his food order going, so I'll catch you later."

She grabbed my arm before I took two

steps. "Since you're not back in study mode yet, consider this: Boomer's band is playing a gig at a club near here. I wondered if you wanted to go with me. You can bring Mad Max."

Mel was into apocalyptic movies and the real Mel Gibson.

"What—tonight?"

She laughed. "Yeah. It's open-mike night, but he doesn't go on until eleven, so I figure if we clean up really fast—another reason I'm mad at Tweedledee and Twiddledum for not showing—we can hoof it over there and maybe catch a song or two. Then we can just hang around and listen to the other bands. It'll be fun."

"Maybe. I have to check with Jude, see if he's interested. I don't know what his plans are." He probably didn't have any, but I didn't know him well enough to know what his likes and dislikes were. I grabbed my menu pad and headed back into the dining room.

Jude was leaning back in his chair. The menu was closed. I had just a moment to fantasize about what it would be like to have dinner here with Jude—dinner as in a date, not free food. I wasn't sure there'd be anything more romantic.

I shoved the fantasy aside and approached the table.

"So what'll you have?" I asked in my very best waitress voice, pencil poised over my pad.

"You weren't kidding about the veggies," he said. "This stuff is *out-of-control* expensive. I can't eat here."

Exactly the way our customers preferred it. For some, eating here was a status symbol.

"Paul is totally okay with it."

Jude shook his head. "I can't do it, Lys. Sorry. I really appreciate the trouble you went to for me, but I just can't." He stood up, leaned in, and kissed my cheek. "You're really sweet, you know that?"

I told myself it was only a kiss on the cheek. It didn't mean anything. But my body wasn't listening. It grew all warm and cozy.

"But I, uh . . . " It was difficult when I couldn't focus, when I kept wanting to replay that kiss, wondering if it had meant something. Mel couldn't be right. Jude and I had met less than twenty-four hours ago—although it seemed like it had been much longer than that. But in a good way.

"What if you could work for it?" I blurted, not even sure where that solution had come from.

But it gave him pause and I could see him considering it. "Doing what?"

"Apparently a couple of the busboys called in sick. You could clear tables?" I said it like a question, because a lot of things had to be factored in. Could he do it? Of course he could. But did he want to do it? And more important, would Paul be okay with it? That was the big question.

Paul was actually very okay with the idea. Quite relieved in fact. I left Jude in his office so Paul could explain things, and went to turn in our dinner order.

All the heady aromas of the kitchen wafted around me as I helped Mel finish getting things ready.

"Orders up!" Chef called out.

I grabbed my dinner and Jude's. He was sitting at the table where I'd left him earlier. He looked extremely happy to see the steak I set before him.

Jude rubbed his hands together. "That looks good."

"What do you want to drink?"

"A beer?"

I shook my head. "Not unless you're twenty-one."

"Where I'm from the drinking age is eighteen, which seems much more civilized."

"Sorry. You'll just have to accept that we're barbarians here. So how about a soda?"

"Sounds good."

I grabbed two sodas and rejoined him at the table. I watched as Jude sliced off a bit of steak. It was kind of strange, because I felt more like a couple with Jude right at that moment than I'd ever felt with Rick.

Rick had never walked me to work. It was a new experience for me, to have so much devoted attention from a guy in so short a time. I told myself that it was just because Jude didn't know anyone else. It could all be different tomorrow.

"Why the long face?" Jude asked.

I jerked out of my morose musings, trying not to acknowledge that Rick had never noticed my subtle moods. I shook my head. "Just lost in thought."

"Thinking about Rick?"

"Sorta. Not really. And I'm sure you don't want to hear about me."

"I enjoy it when you talk about you. I like learning things about you."

Feeling the heat warming my face, I dipped my fork into my potatoes. "So I'm a curiosity?"

"I s'pose, but it's more than that." He ducked his head like maybe he was the one who was now embarrassed.

"Did Rick tell you a lot about me?"

"Not a lot, but enough."

"Why?"

"So I'd feel comfortable asking you for help, I s'pose. Since I don't know anyone else around here."

"But now you know Mel. And Paul. Did he explain everything?"

"Yeah. And he has a white shirt and tie I can borrow. I can't remember the last time I wore a tie. I think it was to my uncle's funeral."

"Oh." I grimaced. "No fun."

"What's no fun?" Mel said, setting her plate down and dropping into the chair across from mine.

"Going to funerals," I said.

"Okay, I can tell we need a serious topic change here. So what is a hot Aussie doing in Vermont?"

Jude gave her his heart-stopping grin. "I'm not sure I've been hot since I arrived in your lovely state."

Mel's laughter was a deep, throaty sound. "Yeah, sure. So did Alyssa tell you that we're going to a club after work?"

Jude raised an eyebrow at me.

"I didn't commit to that," I said. Then I looked back at Jude. "I just haven't had a chance to mention it. It's totally up to you, if you want to go. Her boyfriend plays in a band."

"Live music at a club? Why would I say no?"

I shrugged at Mel. "I believe that's a yes."

"You won't regret it."

"I can't believe you haven't asked me before," I said.

"This is their first gig at a club. They're really nervous. Boomer is convinced something is going to go wrong. You know how they say opposites attract? He's the eternal pessimist; I'm the eternal optimist."

The other employees soon joined us. I made introductions. Jude charmed them all, and he was able to contribute to any conversation. I guessed traveling around and sleeping on other people's couches gave him a vast amount of experience and knowledge.

Unfortunately we weren't leisurely diners, because we were all on a schedule and customers would be arriving any minute. As soon as we finished eating, we cleared the table, taking our dishes to the dishwashing area.

Jude went to Paul's office to get his uniform.

"I like him," Mel said.

"Yeah, I do too."

"So let me ask you. How are you going to be a tour guide *and* go to class?"

"I'll figure something out." I wasn't exactly

sure what. I'd be in class for five hours starting at eight in the morning. Then I needed to study. Of course there was always a chance that after tonight Jude wouldn't need me.

Mel turned her attention toward Paul's office. "Wow!"

Jude was wearing the required white shirt and black tie, and he looked amazing.

Wow indeed, I thought. *Wow indeed.*

Chapter 6

Jude was exceptional. He cleaned and reset the tables in silence, which was part of our restaurant's charm. No one was ever supposed to be disturbed by the work we did. We were quiet and dignified.

Jude also had the energy of two busboys. Once the restaurant closed, cleanup was done in record time.

"You are totally awesome," Mel said to Jude as we walked to the nearby club.

Jude held out his arms as though he was presenting himself onstage. "You're looking at Oz's finest at getting the job done, whatever it is."

And Oz's most modest, apparently, although his confidence in his abilities wasn't a turnoff at all. It just made him more endearing.

"Come on," Mel said, hurrying us toward the club. "I don't hear any music so they must be between acts. We might catch Maximum Output before they start."

"Maximum Output?" I asked.

"That's the name of the band."

"I have a feeling it's not going to be classical music," Jude said.

"Absolutely not," Mel assured him.

We had to show our IDs at the door. Because we were underage, we weren't given a yellow paper bracelet that would have signaled we could buy alcohol.

Jude was, understandably, disappointed. It wasn't that he was obsessed with drinking, but he was accustomed to having a "pint or two" when he went to the clubs. But he was a good sport about the prospect of drinking sodas.

Boomer had claimed a table near the front of the stage. In spite of the cold weather, Boomer was wearing jeans and a T-shirt with the sleeves torn off. His biceps were tattooed with symbols that meant nothing to me. Before tonight he'd always worn his blond hair in a disheveled style, but now it was spiked. He wore braided leather around his neck and both wrists. He looked tough. Quite honestly, I barely recognized him. I guessed he was in performance mode and that was a drastic transition from grad student mode. Introductions were made. Boomer was a guitarist and singer. Tom was the bass guitarist.

"And Zach, our drummer, is running late," Boomer said.

The drums were already in place. Apparently, Boomer had an SUV and he was the one who hauled the drum kit around.

"I could help you out there, mate," Jude said.

"You play drums?" Boomer asked.

"I do indeed."

Boomer slung his arm around Jude and led him toward the stage, giving him instructions, I supposed.

"Well, okay, then," Mel said, dropping into a chair at the table.

"Guess it's a good thing that we came," I said, sitting beside her.

"He is really cute," Mel whispered loudly.

To be heard, all whispers had to be loud.

The place was packed.

"Who? Boomer?" I asked.

"No. Well, yes. Of course. But I meant Jude. So he and Rick swapped couches?" Mel asked.

"Yeah." I rolled my eyes. "Well, except Rick's couch isn't available because Rick forgot to tell Chad, so . . ."

She arched a brow. "So?"

"So . . . Jude's sleeping on my couch."

"Omigod! Are *you* breaking the rules?"

"I know, hard to believe, but"—I leaned conspiratorially toward her—"he is too cute to resist."

"Better watch out, girlfriend. I'm sure Rick meant to give him only the couch."

I decided I needed to fess up about our breakup but at that moment, the drums rumbled through the room.

Boomer stepped up to the mike. "Good evening, dudes and dudettes! We've only got twenty minutes before the next band gets their turn"—he pointed to a table, and five guys threw their arms in the air and cheered—"so let's get started. We're Maximum Output and we're going to blow you away!"

They rocked for twenty minutes, playing familiar songs that established bands had recorded. I figured since they weren't playing original material, Jude was familiar enough with the music to keep up with them—or maybe Boomer had asked him what songs he knew. Whatever. They were great.

About halfway through, Mel stood on her chair and started dancing. Then she looked down at me, like, could I be any more boring? So I climbed on the chair and wiggled around to the hoots and hollers of others in the club. I'd freed my hair from its ponytail before we left work so it was swirling madly around me with my movements.

Some people were dancing in front of the band. Standing on the chair gave me a better view of Jude. He was putting everything he had into the drums, his hair flying around. He was so animated, so into it.

A guy came and sat at our table. Mel mouthed *Zach*. I wondered how he felt watching Jude play—because he was really awesome. Or at least he sounded incredible to me.

Before the last song, Boomer introduced the band members to the audience. He called Jude their guest drummer from Australia—which got a round of cheers. Jude stood up and bowed. He pointed his sticks at me, grinned, and winked.

I waved, feeling as though I was special because of the attention he was showering on me.

When the last song finished, Zach got up to help the band get their equipment off the stage. I sat at the table while Mel went to get sodas for everyone. Since Zach took over the putting away of the drums, Jude was the first to return to the table.

His eyes capturing mine, he bent down, swooping toward me, and I thought, *Omigod! He's going to kiss me! A real kiss this time.*

But at the last second he veered off and just bussed my cheek before dropping into the chair beside me, everything done in one smooth move. I wondered if he played in a band in Australia, if he had groupies that he was accustomed to kissing like that.

Part of me was disappointed that it hadn't been a real kiss, part of me was glad. If he ever did really kiss me, I didn't want it to be quick. Or in a room filled with screaming, temporarily insane people. And why was I even thinking of him really kissing me?

I still kind of had a boyfriend. Did it make me slutty to think about kissing another guy so soon after not officially breaking up with Rick?

I certainly couldn't accuse Jude of not talking. No, he definitely wasn't the strong, silent type. He was the fun-loving, life-is-all-about-having-a-good-time guy.

"You were really good," I told him, leaning near so he could hear me. "Are you part of a band back home?"

"Just me and my mates goofing around, you know? Never really played a gig like this. Just the talent show at school. That sort of thing."

"You looked like a real pro up there."

"I will admit that I have some moves."

Mel brought the drinks over just as the rest of the band was joining us. "Once a waitress, always a waitress," she joked, as everyone took a glass.

Boomer leaned down and planted a kiss on her mouth that had me growing warm. Then he sat and gave his attention to Jude. "Seriously, dude, thanks for helping out tonight."

"No problem."

The next band got set up and then music filled the club again. Jude grabbed my hand. "Come on!"

He pulled me to my feet before I could protest.

"Where are we going? What—"

"We're gonna dance!"

He led me to what passed for the dance area—a narrow strip of flooring where the tables had been pushed back.

"Uh, I don't know how," I confessed.

"You were dancing on the chair," he leaned in and yelled in my ear.

I shook my head. I didn't think it was possible for the music to be any louder. "No, that was just wiggling!"

"It's perfect."

Then he was bobbing, dancing around, the whole time his eyes locked on mine. I realized that even if I looked spastic, which I probably did—thank goodness there were no mirrors hanging around so I could confirm that suspicion—he wouldn't notice because he was concentrating on my gaze, his eyes holding mine as though we were the only two in the place.

I'd had zero dates in high school. Being with Rick was the sum total of my dating experience, and I wasn't certain I could say we'd ever actually had a date. We'd just started . . . hanging out together. Going to the library to study, snuggling on the couch, and watching TV. We'd fallen into habits. I wasn't sure we'd ever fallen in love.

Tonight with Jude wasn't a date. Not in anyone's wildest imagination would it be viewed as a date. We were both here because circumstances had brought us together. Still, I was having a great time—dancing for the first time with a guy. And because it was Jude, who had such a positive outlook on life, I wasn't even self-conscious about my moves—once I got into them anyway. Being with Jude was just fun—it didn't seem so complicated like everything with Rick.

I was having so much fun that I really didn't want the night to end.

But it did end. At two o'clock the last band finished playing and the club closed down.

We were outside, saying good-bye, when Mel said, "Oh, I forgot to tell you. We've got appointments at the spa tomorrow."

Oh, gosh, I'd forgotten all about her wanting to do that. I looked at Jude, then looked at Mel.

"What's this?" Jude asked.

"The ski resort has this to-die-for spa," Mel said. "Alyssa and I have appointments tomorrow for the royal treatment."

"Actually, I don't think tomorrow is going to work for me. Jude doesn't know anyone—"

"He can come with us," Mel said.

Jude and I both released a burst of laughter at the same time. I couldn't see him with a mudpack on his face.

He caught his breath first and said, "You want me to get a manicure? No thank you."

"A massage and facial, then," Mel said.

"That sounds even worse," Jude said.

"You ski?" Boomer asked.

"No," Jude said, "but I'd like to give it a try."

"You can hang out on the slopes with me."

"Sounds great," Jude said. "So we're all set then?"

His gaze had zeroed in on me. I nodded. "Yeah, sure."

"All right. We'll pick you up tomorrow," Mel said. "Do you want a ride home tonight?"

"I'd just as soon walk if you don't mind," Jude said to me.

"I don't mind." The truth was that I needed a little time to come down from the energetic high I was on.

It had started to snow again, huge flakes that floated slowly to the ground. As Jude and I walked along, the streetlights illuminated them and then they disappeared into the darkness.

"Gawd, it's cold!" Jude exclaimed.

Laughing, I said, "You're such a wuss."

I slipped my arm through his, pressing our shoulders close, to create a little friction, a little warmth. And even with the thick coats between us, I felt a zing.

"Well, that helps, a little, I guess," Jude said. "Is it always this cold?"

"Not always. Sometimes it's colder."

We trudged on in silence for a little while, before I said, "I'm really sorry you had to work tonight."

"Not a problem at all."

"But you're on vacation."

"No, I'm on holiday, with very little money in my pockets, and it worked out grand because Paul hired me to work tomorrow night as well. Actually, as long as I'm here. I get a meal and a share of the tips. Besides, what else have I got to do?"

"You're kidding! Paul hired you?"

"Yeah. I thought he seemed like a decent enough bloke. Told him I had to work the same schedule as you, though. Since you're my tour guide and all."

I was feeling like I'd done a pretty decent job today, and tonight.

Still I was feeling a little unsure about things, afraid I was slipping into a complicated situation like I'd had with Rick.

"You know, you don't have to do everything with me," I said awkwardly. "I mean, I can give you my cell phone number and then you can just call me when you need to get into the dorm and I could come down and let you in."

"What if you're out?"

"With classes starting Monday, believe me, I won't be out."

"Probably not a bad idea to get your number, but as long as you're not tired of me, I'd just as soon hang out with you."

"I'm not tired of you at all. I just wanted you to know you had options."

"Now I know."

He grinned at me as though I was silly for even suggesting that he needed options.

Since it was so late when we got back to the dorm, I just unlocked the door and went in, with Jude close on my heels.

As inconspicuously as possible, I shoved him back onto the porch and closed the door in his face. Susan, the dorm monitor, was sitting on the couch in the living room watching *The Holiday*. It was like her favorite movie. But still, who watches a movie at this insane time of night? She looked over her shoulder at me. She had messy black hair that never laid in the same direction so it always looked as though she'd just crawled out of bed.

"Hi, Susan," I said really loudly, hoping Jude would hear and understand what was going on.

"Hey," she said. "You're out late."

"Went to a club, listened to a band." *Not that it's any of your business,* I thought.

"What band?"

"Several actually. It was open-mike night."

"Sounds like fun."

"It was."

She gave a little laugh. "That's out of character for you, isn't it?"

"What can I say? I'm living wild during the break."

"Did you want to watch the movie with me? It's only about fifteen minutes in. I can start it over."

"No, thanks, I'm just going to bed. Night."

I started for the stairs, but took a detour by the door—

"What are you doing?" she asked.

"I just wanted to make sure I locked it."

"It locks automatically."

"Oh, right. I forgot." How was I going to get a message to Jude?

"Were you drinking?" she asked suspiciously.

"What? No. Good night." I hurried up the stairs to the second floor and walked down the hallway to the window that overlooked the front yard. I unlocked it, lifted it up, and stuck my head out the window. "Jude! Jude!"

I tried to use a quiet yelling voice. I didn't know if he'd hear.

Then he was standing on the walkway, looking up at me. I motioned for him to go around to the side of the house.

He nodded and took off. I closed the window and rushed up to my floor. I opened the door to my suite. It was dark. I assumed Stephanie was already asleep.

I went into my room, opened the window, and looked out. Jude was standing beside a large tree. Its branches had kept me awake many a windy night when they scraped against the window.

"Can you climb the tree?" I whispered down.

He gave me a thumbs-up. I watched as he removed his gloves and tucked them inside his jacket. I had my doubts. He was wearing boots . . .

He sat on the ground, pulled them and his socks off, and stuffed them inside his zippered jacket. Then he jumped and grabbed the lowest branch and swung his legs up.

My breath caught as I watched him making his way up the tree. What if he fell? The jig would be up, as they say, because I'd have to get Susan to take him to the emergency room. I couldn't imagine him not being seriously injured if he lost his hold.

He got closer and closer, until he was almost eye-level with me. I heard the awful sound of a branch cracking.

Holding my breath, I watched as he leaped across, his arms, head, and chest coming through the window, the rest of him dangling. I lurched forward, grabbed his jacket, and hauled him in.

He landed on the floor with a thud. His momentum threw me off balance, and I landed on top of him. We were both laughing, more with relief than from anything funny, I think.

"Haven't we done this before?" he joked.

"Not exactly," I said. I knew I should get off him. But I seemed unable to move. Maybe because he'd slipped his hand beneath my jacket.

"Oh, it's warm in there. I think I have frostbite on my fingers and toes."

"I don't think they were exposed long enough for that."

"I had fun tonight," he said quietly.

"Me too." I forced my breathing to slow. "We probably should check your fingers and toes, though. If you hurt yourself you might not have felt it."

"Right." He moved his hands from beneath my jacket and I scrambled off him.

"Is that blood?" I asked, taking his hand.

"Looks like. I must have scraped it on the bark. I probably got blood on your white shirt."

"That doesn't matter. Let's go into the bathroom and take a look."

I made him sit on the edge of the tub. I ran hot water and had him put his feet in.

"Oh, that's nice," he said.

"There is nothing worse than cold feet." I

dampened a washcloth and gently wiped his hand. "Doesn't look bad. I can't believe Susan was up."

I spread some antibacterial salve over the scrape.

"She's the wicked witch of the dorm, right?"

I peered up at him. His eyes were so green. And he was watching me, not looking at his wound.

"She's not that bad. She's just a stickler about the rules. Sorry you had to come in through the window."

"Not a problem. It was an adventuresome way to get in, wasn't it?"

"You like adventure."

"It's in my blood."

"Really?" I thought for a moment. "Australia was a prison colony or something like that, right? A couple of hundred years ago?"

"Yeah. Early part of the nineteenth century. The British sent convicts over."

"So were your ancestors convicts?"

He nodded. "My mum is into genealogy. She traced our origins and discovered that our first Australian ancestor was indeed a thief."

"Really?" I asked.

"Yeah. Apparently, he stole a good many ladies' hearts." He winked at me.

I laughed. "Do you take anything seriously?"

"As little as possible. Life is too short for serious." He leaned toward me and skimmed his fingers along my cheek. "Although I think there are some things worth getting serious over."

My heart did a little stutter. I'd just ended one relationship—well, kind of. Was I ready to jump into another? *Should* I jump into another?

"You know we should probably get to bed," I stammered.

His gaze intensified.

"I mean, I'll get to bed, you'll get to couch," I clarified.

I scrambled up. "I have some bandages if you want to put them over the scrape."

"It'll be fine." He pulled his feet out of the tub and wrapped them in a towel. "Maybe I *should* consider going to the spa."

I glanced at him and smiled. "You really don't strike me as the spa type."

He dropped the towel into the hamper.

"What about *your* feet?" he asked quietly. "Are they hurting?"

"Yeah, they are. How'd you know?"

"'Cause I saw how hard you worked tonight. I know you're getting that massage tomorrow, but if you like I can rub them now."

My breath hitched with the thought.

"A girl can never get her feet rubbed too much, but you don't have to—"

"I want to. I wouldn't have offered otherwise. I owe you a lot," he said. "It's a small way to pay you back."

Payback. Why was I disappointed? Why was I wanting his reason to be more personal?

Still, the truth was any reason for a foot rub was good enough for me.

"Okay. Yeah. Sure. Just for a minute. But I think I'll change out of my work clothes first."

"Sure. I'll meet you on the couch."

He walked out of the room. A hot Aussie was going to rub my feet. All right!

Not giving him a chance to change his mind, I quickly undressed and threw on sweats, washed my feet, and put on some socks.

Jude was already sitting on the couch when

I went into the living room. I was suddenly experiencing a touch of nervousness.

"Do you want anything to eat or drink?"

"No." He patted the seat cushion. "Just sit down." He patted his thighs. "Put your feet here."

"Okay." Sitting and twisting around, with my back against the side of the couch, I put my thick socked feet on his lap.

He didn't waste any time. He started rubbing my feet, and I released a little moan. "That feels good." I opened my eyes and looked at him. He was watching my face, not my feet. "Shouldn't you be tired?"

"I s'pose, except that it's daytime in Australia."

"Your schedule must really be messed up."

"Not too bad. I've never needed much sleep. And so far, I've never been hit with jet lag when I travel."

I picked up one of the decorative pillows from the floor, put it in my lap, and started picking at a loose thread. "Would you like to, uh, date someone while you're here? I mean, I could probably set you up with someone." I wasn't sure who, but surely I could find someone.

When he didn't say anything, I lifted my gaze to his.

"Not really, no."

I felt a sense of relief—and panic, because he was studying me so intently.

He continued, "It's probably not such a good idea for me to get involved with someone, since I'm not here very long. Besides, I'd rather just hang out with you."

My heart sank a bit. Had I been misreading him this whole time?

"But—" I stopped.

"But?" he prodded.

"I'm not going to have a lot of time when classes start."

His hands stilled and my feet had an absurd desire to wiggle and regain his attention. "I have fun with you, so whatever time you have that's fine with me."

"I don't know if I've met anyone like you before."

"I should think not. As far as I know, I don't have a twin."

I pulled back my feet and scooted toward the

center of the couch. "I really had fun tonight."

"I did too." Reaching out, he tucked my hair behind my ear, then brought it forward again. "I don't think I've seen eyes as blue as yours. They're almost violet."

"My dad calls them Elizabeth Taylor eyes. It's not a very common shade of blue apparently."

"They're gorgeous." His gaze dropped to my lips.

And what could I say about them? Nothing except that they were tingling in anticipation.

He very, very slowly moved toward me—

Stephanie opened her door and I jerked back so fast that I nearly gave myself whiplash. Until that moment I hadn't even realized that I'd moved toward Jude.

"Oh, hey," Stephanie said. "I thought I heard you."

What could she have heard? We'd been quiet, talking low.

"I'm sorry. We were trying to be quiet."

"It wouldn't have taken much. I can't sleep."

She plopped down on the couch right between Jude and me—as though there was room between us for someone to sit.

She released a burdensome sigh. "My best friend called tonight. She's getting married."

"Isn't that cause for celebration?" Jude asked.

She scoffed. "You'd think. But she wants to get married in June and I wanted to go to Europe in June."

Over her head, Jude and I exchanged glances. *She was losing sleep over this?*

"So . . . go in July," I suggested.

"I guess that would work. It's just not what I was planning."

"You could skip the wedding."

She looked at me as though she wanted to ask what planet I came from. "I'm the maid of honor. And that's another thing. The groom's brother is going to be the best man. And he's an old boyfriend, so that is going to be totally awkward."

She turned her attention to Jude. "What do you think I should do?"

"To be honest, I'm not sure I see what the problem is."

"I thought you'd be different because you're

from Australia. But I guess guys everywhere are the same."

She sat there, staring at the turned-off TV, as though she had no plans of ever leaving, which left things up to me.

I gave an exaggerated yawn. "Well, guess since this is Jude's bed, and it's after three in the morning, we should get to ours."

I got up. When she didn't move, I nudged her shoulder. "Come on, Stephanie."

She got up, none too happily it appeared, and shuffled back to her bedroom. Then she waited in the doorway for me to make my exit.

"Night, Jude," I said.

"G'night."

I walked to my bedroom, stood in the doorway, and looked at Stephanie. Like characters in a romantic comedy both after the same guy, we watched each other as we went into our rooms and closed the door.

"What was that all about?" I murmured as I crawled into bed.

I reached over and turned out the lamp.

When I went to sleep, I dreamed that I was

at the spa getting my massage. The massage therapist spoke with an Aussie accent. Probably because he wasn't Hans.

He was Jude.

Chapter 7

"Okay, so spill it. What is the real deal with you and the hot Aussie?"

Mel's question immediately destroyed the Zen state I'd achieved during the incredible massage that Levy—not Hans, not Jude—had delivered. Ladies with names that I forgot had handled the nail treatments and facials. After enjoying finger sandwiches, we were now in the sauna and I was beginning to think that I probably didn't have any bones remaining in my body.

Suddenly I went all stiff and sat up, surprised I didn't pull a muscle. "What do you mean?"

"Duh. The two of you last night? The kiss he gave you before he headed for the slopes?"

"It was a kiss on the cheek. It's what Aussies do."

"Yeah. Uh-huh. Sure. It's only a matter of time before that kiss lands on your mouth—if it hasn't already."

I adjusted the towel wrapped around me. I felt very exposed. "You think?"

"I'm really not being judgmental here, but is it fair to Rick—"

"We're not together," I blurted.

"I know that. He's in Australia, but that doesn't mean—"

"No, no." I took a deep breath. "We sorta temporarily broke up."

Her eyes widened in surprise, then reflected concern, as though she couldn't figure out what she should be feeling or what her reaction should be. "When? Why? Why didn't you say something? And what do you mean temporarily? You either broke up or you didn't."

I shrugged, turned my back into the corner, and brought my feet up to the wooden bench, tucking the towel where it needed tucking to keep me from flashing anyone. Three other women were in the sauna but they were on the other side, far enough away not to hear our conversation.

"It was right before finals. I didn't say anything because honestly I felt like a failure. My parents met in middle school, have been together forever. Rick was my first boyfriend and I got it wrong. I'm starting to think I got it very badly wrong."

She angled her head thoughtfully. "He was never good enough for you anyway."

I groaned. "See. That's another reason I didn't want to say anything. Because we *might* get back together, and if you say stuff like that, it'll make it awkward to hang out with you."

"Okay, I won't say anything." Silence resulted for all of three seconds. "I have to say, if you don't mind me saying, that's a half-assed breakup, and they never come to any good. You should make a clean break. Call him in Australia and tell him it's over. Then you can concentrate on Jude."

Sighing, I closed my eyes and leaned my head back, desperate to reclaim the calm.

"There's nothing wrong with a relationship

not being forever," Mel said quietly. "A lot can be said for a relationship that's for now."

I opened my eyes. "Is that what you and Boomer have? A for-now thing?"

"Probably not. I mean, I'm seriously nuts about the guy. But you and Jude . . . you like him, right?"

"Oh yeah."

"It's obvious he likes you."

"But he doesn't take anything seriously."

"Unlike you, who takes everything way too seriously."

I gave her a rueful grin. "He's only here for a short time. It doesn't make sense to get . . . involved. It just seems like he's a heartbreak waiting to happen."

"So you're just going to be his—what? Tour guide?"

She said it as though it was a thought too disgusting to even contemplate.

"I don't know, Mel. I guess I've always expected to have what my parents had—you meet the guy and it's forever."

"Nice fairy tale. And I'm not knocking it. It's just that if the prince turns out to be a frog, it might be worth it to have a little while with another prince, just to keep things in perspective."

A little while was all we had time for since the three of us had to get to work that evening. Mel and I were sitting in front of the massive fireplace in the lodge lobby, roasting our toes, when the guys caught up with us.

Jude dropped down on the coffee table in front of me. I wasn't sure if his huge smile was a result of seeing me or a reflection of the fun he'd had on the slopes. Things between us weren't awkward but there was an awareness now that I wasn't quite sure how to handle. All morning we'd been surreptitiously glancing at each other as though we were fencing, waiting for the other person to make the first move.

I smiled in response to his. "How'd it go?"

"It totally rocked. You and I should give it a go sometime."

"He caught on really fast," Boomer said, before I could respond. He was sitting on the arm of Mel's chair, leaning toward her as though he really just wanted to curl around her.

"Really?" I teased, making it sound like I thought it improbable. Anything to keep the conversation going while I tried to figure out my next move.

"Oh yeah. It's all about keeping your balance, isn't it? Like surfing. Although actually, surfing is a little less dependable because you're always at the mercy of the waves. You never know what they'll do. Here you have a trail."

"I thought you only couch surfed," I joked.

"Nah, I'm all about catching the waves. Well, that and scuba diving. To be honest, anything involving water. I live right there on the coast."

"He was telling me about a shark attack—"

"Omigod!" I blurted before Boomer could finish the tale. "You were attacked by a shark?"

"No, no. But he was swimming toward me. Looked in my eyes." Jude pointed two fingers at his face. Then turned his fingers toward me. "I looked in his. He just swam away. Mutual respect."

Just lucky! I shuddered. "That gives me goose bumps."

"You shouldn't have told her that," Mel said.

"Now she'll never go in the water again."

"I'm not that bad," I insisted.

"In case you haven't figured it out, she is Miss Cautious."

Jude winked at me. I wondered if he was thinking what I was. Since he'd come into my life, I wasn't nearly as cautious as I used to be.

We checked out the lunch menu at the lodge restaurant and decided it wasn't Rachael Ray–worthy, so we hit a sandwich shop in the resort village.

After we ate our sandwiches and downed hot chocolate, we walked around. Somehow my hand ended up in Jude's. I wasn't sure if he'd made the move or I had, but it seemed so natural.

Quaint little shops dotted the village.

"I probably need to start thinking about souvenirs for the family and a couple of my mates," Jude said when we stopped to look through the window of a candy shop. "Fudge made with real Vermont butter," he murmured, reading the sign posted in the window. "Is there something special about Vermont butter?"

"Everything about Vermont is special."

Jude smiled. "I s'pose you have a point."

"I'm going in," Mel said.

"And she may never come out," Boomer joked.

"Yes, I will." She grabbed his arm. "You'll make me leave before I buy too much candy."

Shaking his head, he let her pull him inside. "It's her weakness" was all he got out before the door closed.

"Did you want to go inside?" I asked.

"I'm thinking fudge wouldn't hold up well as a gift. I won't be home for a month."

"We have teddy bears."

"I can get something made in China back home."

I gave him a playful nudge. "No, no, these are Vermont-famous teddy bears. Made right here. Not that I think your *mates* would want one, but your sister might."

"Yeah, she might at that. Girls never get too old for stuffed animals, do they?"

"I haven't reached that point yet," I said, as we strolled over to a shop with bears and souvenir items displayed in the window. I could see our distorted reflections in the glass. I stood just below his shoulder.

"Now these are fancy," he said.

The bears were dressed in different outfits, some representing various occupations.

"So what does Marla do?" I asked, somewhat nonchalantly, I thought.

"She's a teacher. On summer break now."

"Summer?"

He grinned. "Yeah, it's summer Down Under."

I shook my head. "Oh, right. That just seems so weird to me."

"Well, freezing my bum off this time of year seems weird to me. Ah, look, there's a doctor bear. It's even got a stethoscope. I should get that for you."

"What are you talking about? You don't need to get me a souvenir."

"No, but a thank-you gift might be nice, don't you think?"

"Nice, yes, but absolutely not necessary."

"Come on, Lys. I know you weren't planning to spend your holiday entertaining me. You've been a good sport about it."

Okay, I was thinking I'd never enjoyed being with anyone so much and he was seeing me as a good sport. So was I more than a tour guide or not?

"Seriously, don't even worry about it. Hey, why don't you get your mates some maple syrup? It won't go bad before you get it home." I felt like doing some sort of hand motions to reveal various souvenir options.

"You all right?" he asked.

"Oh yeah, sure."

Although the truth was that suddenly I felt like I just wanted to get away. I'd begun to think we were drifting into romantic territory. But maybe I'd misread last night—and the hand-holding today.

"Hey, mate!"

Jude's sudden words brought me out of my thoughts. It sounded like he'd just seen someone he knew. I swung around. It was an older couple.

"Would you mind taking a picture of us?" he asked, extending his camera.

"Oh, sure," the man said.

Jude stepped over and gave quick instructions for his camera. Then he stepped back, slung his arm around me, and hauled me in close against his side. "Smile."

As though I needed that suggestion. My immediate reaction to being nestled against him was to smile wide enough that my jaws might begin to ache if he held me too long.

The man snapped the photo. "I think that did it."

Jude took back the camera and looked at the photo. "Oh yeah, that's great."

He turned it toward me. "Keeper?"

We were both smiling brightly. Who looked that happy souvenir shopping? But we did. "Keeper."

"Excellent." He turned back to the couple. "Thanks ever so much."

The couple told us to have fun, before walking off. I was left to wonder if Jude ever met a stranger he didn't like.

Jude passed on buying any souvenirs. On the way back to the dorm, I'd gone kind of quiet, not sure what I wanted. I hadn't wanted to be a tour guide at all, but I'd grown into it, and now suddenly I wanted to be more than a tour guide—and that thought terrified me. Because like I'd told Mel, it could only lead to heartache. I thought I could fall for this hot Aussie. Then he'd be gone and I'd be—what? Back with Rick? Or not back with Rick, but dreaming about Jude?

Later in my room, as I yanked my hair into a ponytail, I reminded myself that I was supposed to be thinking about Rick, trying to figure out if I wanted us to get back together. But the truth was if he called and asked me right then, I knew deep down that I would have said no, which I guessed said it all.

When I was finished getting dressed, I let Jude have the bedroom so he could get ready.

I was pacing around the couch when Stephanie returned from another day on the slopes. Her cheeks were ruddy, and she was wearing her pink ski pants and matching jacket.

"Hey," she said. "Where's the hot Aussie?"

I jerked my thumb toward my room. "Getting ready for work." I gave her the CliffsNotes version of how that had come about.

"Wow. Not much of a vacation." She shed

her coat and hung it on the coat rack near the door.

"It's just a few hours each night. And we're off the next three."

"Still." She dropped down onto the couch. "I'm wiped. We skied all day."

Stephanie wasn't experiencing the money crisis that I was. She studied me, angling her head one way and then another, as though I was one of those holograms that changed scenes based on the way you looked at it.

"What?" I finally snapped.

"Is there something going on between you and Jude? There is, isn't there?"

"No." Not yet anyway, but maybe . . .

"Okay. Just so you know, I'm going home for a few days." Stephanie frowned. "Probably just a couple. My mom drives me nuts after about ten minutes, but I have to make the obligatory trip home or she'll disown me."

"Which means your bed will be available."

"How do you figure?"

"You won't be using it. You could let Jude borrow it."

"I don't want a stranger sleeping in my bed."

Who was she? One of the three bears?

"He's not a stranger. You know him."

"Not really."

My mouth dropped open. Had she not practically snuggled up against him on the couch last night, taking over *my* snuggling position?

"More than you know whoever slept in your bed last semester."

"I thoroughly sanitized the mattress, the room, and the bath."

"He could sleep on the other bed." She had a private room. Her parents paid big bucks so she wouldn't have to share.

Stephanie shook her head. "Sorry. I'll be locking the door when I leave. Let him sleep on Sheli's bed."

That *was* an option. I knew Sheli wouldn't mind. But there was the matter of me being in the room when Jude was in the room . . .

"What if *I* used your room?" I suggested.

"Nope. He's your problem, not mine. I'm not going to be inconvenienced."

"He's not a *problem*, and how will you be inconvenienced when you're not even here?"

"You don't understand. I can't deal with

someone living in my space—even if I'm not there. It's the reason I don't have a roommate."

"Fine." My suitemate *was* mental. "How about leaving your keycard—"

"No, no, no."

The door to my bedroom opened and Jude stepped out. I felt as though all the air had been sucked right out of the room. Jude was wearing the required white shirt and tie. He'd also shaved and styled his hair so it didn't look disheveled. I'd thought he looked gorgeous before. But this was . . .

"Wow. Don't you clean up nice," Stephanie said.

"Stephanie!" I scowled at her.

"What?" She unfolded her body from the couch like a cat ending its nap in the sun. "He does."

She disappeared into her room. Even though her room was off-limits, I was relieved she was leaving. I wouldn't have to keep peering into the room to see if she was decent.

"Ignore her," I told him. "Although you do look amazing."

"I prefer to totally relax on holiday, but I

was starting to look a bit scruffy. And with the job and all, well, I thought maybe I should tidy up a bit." He rubbed his hands together as though we were going on another adventure. "Shall we be off?"

"Absolutely."

No doubt about it. The Chalet had just acquired one hot busboy.

Chapter 8

Sunday night wasn't quite the madhouse of the night before. One of the AWOL busboys—Kent—returned. The other had supposedly tumbled down "the stairs" and broken his leg.

"More likely the ski slope," Mel mumbled.

I said nothing, because I figured she was right. And honestly I wasn't in any mood to complain when Jude was now part of the crew, with free eats privileges. Plus it was simply more fun having him around, winking at me and smiling for no apparent reason.

"Does that guy think we're having a contest here?" Kent asked me at the doorway into the kitchen, as Jude reached a recently vacated table and proceeded to clear it. "He's like super busguy or something."

"I think it's called initiative. You know,

seeing what needs to be done and doing it."

Kent scowled at me. "So where'd he come from?"

"Australia."

"I got that. Is he going to school here? I mean, it's going to wear me out keeping up with him."

"Don't worry, he'll be leaving in two or three weeks," I said, not at all surprised by the disappointment that thought brought me. I was enjoying Jude's company. He even cleared the tables with flair. I could stand there and watch him all night, but I had a table that needed my attention.

I went over to the candlelit table where some regulars were waiting. Dr. Campbell was one of the deans at the university. He was with his wife and two daughters. Hailey, the older one, went to the university and was in my calculus class. She went through boyfriends the way I went through a bag of chips.

I'd just taken her sister's order, when Hailey set down her menu to tell me what she wanted. But she froze, then whispered, "Omigod. This may have just become my favorite restaurant."

I glanced in the direction she was looking, not surprised to discover that Jude had moved to a closer table and thus, snagged her attention.

It occurred to me that if Jude came over and talked or grinned at Hailey that she'd have him pull up a chair to join them. As a matter of fact, she'd probably offer him *her* couch—if not her bed.

Why was I irritated with Hailey for noticing what a gorgeous guy Jude was? Any girl would notice. I'd never felt this possessive when girls looked at Rick. But the truth was that what I was beginning to feel for Jude was very different from what I'd felt for Rick. On so many levels. It was scary but also thrilling.

Dr. Campbell cleared his throat, snapping me back to my duties.

"Your order, miss," I said formally.

"I'll have him," she said, pointing at Jude.

"Hailey, don't be silly and it's rude to point," her father said, clearly frustrated that it was taking so long to get their order taken.

Hailey just rolled her eyes and looked up at me. "He's new, isn't he? I don't remember ever seeing him working here before."

"We're not allowed to discuss the staff," I told her, hoping it sounded like it might be an actual rule. I didn't want her anywhere near Jude. I was feeling protective of him. Or was it jealousy?

"All right, fine." She pouted for a second, then gave me her order. She had "I plan to be difficult" written all over her face.

After taking everyone's order, I headed back to the kitchen via Jude, who was pushing an aluminum cart of dirty dishes.

"I think you're probably the only guy around here who looks like he actually enjoys clearing tables," I said in a low, dignified voice. The Chalet was all about being dignified.

He grinned at me and leaned low. I smelled the wonderful scent of him. "Keeps me busy. Makes the time fly until you're off work and we can do something."

I wondered what he had in mind. Were we going to finish what we might have been starting last night?

"Are you blushing?" he asked.

"What? No."

"Does it bother you—what I said?"

"Of course not, but I need to get this order turned in."

I hurried into the kitchen, nearly running into Mel as she was coming out.

"Kent quit. Can you believe it? I've heard of spring fever. But winter fever? What is it with these guys and their sudden lack of enthusiasm for work?"

She carried her tray into the dining room before I could answer. Not that I had an answer. Or really cared.

My thoughts were taken up with Jude and wondering what we might do after work.

"This is *so* not what I ordered," Hailey said after I brought out their food.

"Filet mignon, medium rare," I said, confirming her request by looking at the order slip.

"Right. And this is *so* not rare."

Looking at Hailey's steak in the dim romantic candlelight of the restaurant, I could have sworn it was medium rare.

"What is it exactly?" I asked. I truly wasn't being a smart-ass. I just wasn't certain if she thought it was cooked too much or too little.

She gave me a look that said I was too clueless to breathe the same air that she did. "Overdone."

I plastered on my I-will-be-a-charming-waitress-no-matter-how-*uncharming*-the-guests-may-be smile. "I'll return it to the kitchen and have the chef prepare another one for you."

"Make it quick, because I'm starving."

I wasn't sure how she could be. They'd already eaten their salads and two baskets of rolls. Still I took the plate back into the kitchen. I placed it on the counter. "Hailey doesn't like her steak," I announced.

"Hailey never likes her steak," Chef muttered. "Come back in three."

I grabbed a pitcher of water, so I could do a quick run-through, filling water glasses. I was heading for the door when it swung open and Jude backed in, pulling a cart with him. He nodded toward the pitcher I was holding. "Leave that. I'll see to it."

"No, I can—"

"Alyssa! Order up!"

I nodded at Jude, setting the pitcher

aside. "Okay, thanks. Just be sure you step back from the table so no cold water splashes on them."

"I worked at a restaurant back home for a while. I think I've got it."

"Oh, that explains your bussing skills."

He gave me his usual grin. "My bussing skills?"

"Yeah, I'm afraid you intimidated Kent."

"Didn't mean to. Just doing my job." He winked at me, before pushing the cart into the dishwashing area.

I returned to the counter to pick up the food waiting on me. It wasn't Hailey's steak; it was another order. The people at that table were much easier to please, nodding their heads with approval at the condition of their steaks and seafood. When I returned to the kitchen, Hailey's steak was ready.

"Any bets on whether or not she accepts this one?" Mel asked, preparing a basket of rolls for one of her tables.

"No. She's trying to make a point, because I wouldn't give her details about Jude."

"So give her the details. Tell her he's spoken for."

"But he's not."

She arched a brow. "Do not let her think he's available. She'll dig her claws into him and not let go."

"We all have such a high opinion of her."

"I had a class with her, and she is not pleasant."

As I approached Hailey's table, I felt my mouth go dry. Jude was standing at the table, water pitcher in hand, talking with Hailey. I wondered if she was the reason that he'd offered to do a water run, if he'd wanted an excuse to talk with her. Had I been a fool to think something was developing between Jude and me? Obviously, because here he was flirting with another girl.

He liked meeting people. He'd met me and now he was meeting someone else. I wasn't special. I was just good enough until something better came along.

If Paul spotted him, Jude might lose his complimentary evening meals. He really wasn't supposed to be bothering the guests. Although judging by the look of adoration—and ownership—on Hailey's face, she wasn't considering his attention a bother.

I set the plate down with a clatter—not something I normally did—and caught everyone's attention. I should have apologized but I was suddenly in a prickly mood. "Here you are. If you'll please cut into your steak and see if it's cooked to your satisfaction."

She scowled up at me, before doing as I asked. Then she tilted up her nose and gave me a fake smile. "Sorry. Still too cooked."

"Caw, really?" Jude asked. "That's just the way I like it."

Hailey swiveled her head around to look at him, a tiny pleat appearing between her brows. I tried to get Jude's attention to wave him off. A confrontation with Hailey wasn't pretty. Sometimes I just wanted to smack her parents and ask why they let her get away with such rude behavior.

But Jude either didn't see my motions or he was ignoring me. His attention was all on Hailey. I had a feeling he might be contemplating changing tour guides.

"See, a nice section of red there in the middle," Jude said. "Then a bit of pink, followed by brown to hold in the flavors. Perfection. If you've never tasted it prepared like that, I highly recommend you give it a go."

"Really?" she asked. "Really, this is the way you like it?"

"Absolutely. And you know who else eats his steak prepared like that? Hugh Jackman."

"How do you know that?" she asked suspiciously, and I thought Jude had blown it.

"I worked in a restaurant in Australia. He came in all the time. And that's just the way he ordered his steak prepared. Exactly like yours."

Her eyes had grown wide. Her sister's mouth was hanging open.

"Well," Hailey said. "If Hugh Jackman prefers it this way . . ." She let her voice trail off as she smiled at him, then looked up at me. "It's fine. My compliments to the chef."

"Fantastic. I'll let him know. Is there anything else I can get anyone?" I asked the table in general.

My question was met with head shakes, so

I walked away. When I glanced back, Jude had wandered over to another table and was filling glasses there. If not for him, I'd have probably been taking steaks back to the chef all night.

"I owe you big-time," I told Jude.

The restaurant doors were locked. All the customers had left. I was helping Jude clear off the last few tables that had dishes on them.

"For what?" he asked.

"For handling Hailey and the rare-steak situation." It sounded like the title to a children's book.

"She gave me her number so I could ring her up," he said matter-of-factly.

I felt that funny twinge. "So are you gonna call her?"

"She's not my type. I don't like trouble-makers."

I felt an odd sense of relief.

"She probably has a much more comfort-able couch than I do," I told him. "I bet she'd make it available to you."

"But she's not *comfortable* to be around."

His words returned my good humor. "So

you really waited on Hugh Jackman?"

He appeared stunned. Then he grimaced and made a little moan. "Did I say Hugh Jackman earlier? Gawd, I'm always doing that. No, no. Hugh Jack*son*. Big bloke. Used cars salesman . . . "

I started to laugh.

"Always wearing these atrocious plaid jackets."

I was laughing so hard I felt tears in my eyes.

"What? You don't believe me?" he asked.

"I can't believe you lied."

"I didn't lie. It was an honest mistake."

"Whatever. I appreciated it." I got very serious. "I don't know if Paul would have appreciated it."

"What's he gonna do? Fire me? When all I'm doing is helping out? You worry too much."

"Okay, stop hogging the hottie," Mel said as she came up to the table. She'd already removed her tie and unbuttoned the top three buttons on her shirt.

"Has the band got another gig?" Jude asked her.

"Nope. Maybe next week. I'll let you know.

Meanwhile, I'm throwing a little party at my place tomorrow night. I expect you guys to be there."

Jude looked at me, arched a brow.

"We're in," I said.

"Great." Mel took my arm. "Come on. I'll draw you a map to my place."

She seemed incredibly intent on hauling me to the kitchen.

"I know where you live," I said, nearly tripping over my feet.

"You don't think that excuse was the real reason I wanted to get you away from him, do you?"

"You wanted to get me away from him?"

"Just for a sec."

We stopped on the dining room side of the swinging door that led into the kitchen.

"There's really a definite connection between you two, between you and Jude," Mel said. "I just thought I should point it out again because I have the impression that sometimes you're blind where guys are concerned."

"I don't know, Mel. He's only going to be here for two or three weeks."

"Then make the best of them, girlfriend."

❊ ❊ ❊

It was after midnight. I was sitting on my bed, my legs curled beneath me, while I sipped hot chocolate. Jude was at my computer, uploading his pictures to some picture-sharing account that he had.

We'd both dressed down, putting away our Chalet uniforms and slipping into comfy sweats. His hair was all tousled from his shower. He looked rumpled and adorable.

I glanced over at Sheli's bed, considered . . . no.

"I have class tomorrow morning," I told him.

He looked up from the computer. "What time?"

"Eight. I'll be back around two."

"First day of class? They never keep you the whole time."

"Yeah, but this is an entire semester crammed into two weeks. I think they probably will."

"Why would you do that?" He sounded truly baffled.

"I'm looking at years of schooling. Whatever I can get done sooner, the better."

He shook his head. "You'll burn yourself out."

"I like studying."

He scrutinized me. "Can I ask you something? But I don't want you to think I'm being nosy."

I felt a little fissure of dread go through me. "Sure."

The word came out hesitantly.

"While I've been sitting here, uploading my pictures, I noticed this little grid." He pointed at my dry erase board where I blocked out my time. "Do you account for every hour of every day?"

I set the mug aside, unfolded my body, and walked over to the desk. "Pretty much. It's the only way I can get everything done." It was a habit I'd borrowed from my mom. Growing up, she'd enrolled me in every extracurricular activity that she could make time for—to give me an opportunity to experience everything, decide my own likes and dislikes.

"What about spontaneity?"

His face was illuminated by the glow of the computer. For some reason, we'd decided to leave the lights off except for the low-wattage lamp by my bed. It created an intimacy.

"I make time for that. See?" I touched a blank square. "I allow an hour—"

"An hour?" He started laughing.

"It works for me, okay?" It irritated me that he didn't understand my system. Or worse, that he was ridiculing it.

He stopped laughing. "Okay."

"I can be spontaneous."

He grinned. "Really?"

"Yeah." I tensed, relaxed, went for the unexpected. "How would you like to sleep on Sheli's bed tonight?"

His gaze shifted past me to the bed. "You mean in here?"

"Well, yeah, that's where the bed is."

His gaze came back to me. "What about Stephanie?"

"She has her own bed."

He laughed. "No, I mean, won't she think—"

"I don't care what she thinks. She suggested it, actually." As soon as I said it, I wished I hadn't. Why hadn't I just taken credit for the idea? I'd thought about it too. I just hadn't voiced it aloud.

"It'd certainly be more comfortable," he said.

"Okay, then. Great." I was going to be sleeping in my sweats tonight.

Jude finished uploading his pictures. Then we went through the ritual of getting ready for bed. Neither of us talked. An awkwardness had suddenly emerged, and I was sort of wishing I could take back the offer.

Finally, we were each in our respective beds and I switched off the light.

We seemed even quieter then. I wasn't sure I'd be able to sleep.

"Lys?" Jude whispered in the darkness.

"Yeah?"

"G'night."

The bed squeaked as he rolled over.

I released the breath I didn't know I'd been holding. "Good night."

I rolled over too. And smiled.

Chapter 9

Jude and I had survived the night, sleeping in the same room. I knew he'd survived because I could hear him breathing when I sneaked out of the room to go to class, trying really hard not to disturb him.

"So you're going to actually cook something?" Jude asked dubiously.

We were walking down the baking aisle at the grocery store that afternoon. He'd insisted on coming with me, even though I'd reminded him there were more exciting things to do in Vermont. He'd given me a look that said he thought I was silly for even suggesting that.

"I can cook," I said, semi-insulted. "And since I'm making something to take to the party"—I grabbed a bag of sugar and Karo syrup—"I might as well prepare something for lunch. So what do you want?"

"What's your specialty?"

"Beef stroganoff. Lots of carbs and things that aren't good for you."

"Sounds like something I'd love." He grabbed a brownie mix and tossed it into the cart where it landed on top of the muffin mix and cake mix he'd already thrown in.

"I didn't think you liked sweet things."

"Not crazy about fudge."

"How do you feel about divinity?"

"To be honest, I've never had it, but if that's what you're making, I'm sure I'll love it."

What was I trying to prove here? I wasn't Suzy Homemaker, and divinity was a lot of work: boiling, beating, setting.

"How about dips? You like dips?"

My grandmother had sent me a dip recipe that was super easy to make. Cream cheese, Rotel, onions, and dried beef. Mix it up and voilà!

"Anything that a chip goes into is good by me."

And apparently he'd never met a chip he didn't like. I didn't know why I hadn't thought to bring him to a grocery store before. He was apparently a junk food junkie. We had three bags of chips, a couple of packages of cookies, and some peanut butter crackers in our cart.

"Have you considered that we have to walk back to the dorm carrying all this stuff?" I asked.

He swept his arms around and bent slightly, doing one of those poses that bodybuilders use to show off their muscles. Not that any muscles were showing since he was wearing his jacket. Still, the silliness of it in the grocery store made me laugh.

He loaded various sodas and juices into the cart. I was beginning to wonder if I could have been a worse hostess, not considering that he might get the munchies.

Get over it, Alyssa. You were totally unprepared for a guest.

As we neared the checkout line, Jude plucked a bouquet of half a dozen red and white carnations out of a barrel.

"I need these for my girl."

My heart did a little flip. Had I become his girl? I had this insane vision of him going down on one knee in the middle of the grocery store to present them to me.

"Your girl?" I stammered.

"Yeah, Molly."

My heart squeezed. How had I missed him meeting Molly? Then I thought of last night at The Chalet. . . .

"You mean Hailey?"

His brow furrowed. "Gawd, no. Why would you think that? We'll stop by and see Molly on the way back."

"Where does she live?"

"Not far."

He helped me put our groceries on the conveyor belt, then handed me some cash. "This should take care of my share. If you'll handle the actual paying, I need to take care of something."

"Yeah, sure." Suddenly he was Mr. Mysterious. And okay, maybe I was a little disappointed that the flowers weren't for me.

I watched his long strides take him toward Customer Service. Maybe there was a special Australian product he wanted them to order.

He certainly wasn't shy about asking for what he wanted.

As I waited for our items to be rung up and bagged, it seemed like our quick trip to the store for a few items had morphed into stocking up in case of an apocalyptic event where we were the only remaining survivors. Not that there wasn't some appeal to the idea of being totally alone with Jude.

So again, who was this Molly chick?

I paid for the groceries and began pushing the cart toward Customer Service. No matter how buff and strong Jude was, I didn't really see how we were going to carry all these bags home.

Wearing a big grin, Jude made his way back over to me. "I'll push."

"Um, actually, we need to carry."

"No, we don't. I got permission from the manager for us to borrow the cart. Great one, the manager."

"I bet you used your Aussie charm on him."

He winked. "On her."

I found myself smiling. Everyone fell in love

with Jude. Was what I was feeling for him any different?

Was it the novelty of Jude that made me wonder what it might be like to be more than a tour guide? Or was I falling for him? And had he fallen for Molly?

"So where does this Molly live?" I asked again.

"The park."

"What? She's a homeless person?" Not that I'd ever seen any homeless people at the park.

Jude laughed. "No, she's the snowgirl we made."

He'd had more of a hand in making her than I had, but if he wanted to give me credit, who was I to complain?

I was really hoping she'd still be there. I knew she hadn't melted. Our weather hadn't gone above freezing. But sometimes kids got carried away and destroyed things.

But when we arrived, not only was she still there, but apparently she'd gotten married! There was a snowman beside her and three little snowkids in front of them.

Jude was grinning broadly and I was

laughing. Apparently Jude's creation had caught someone's attention and a community project had been born.

"She's got a family now," he said.

I was still laughing when he extended the flowers to me. My heart just sort of rolled over and started to melt.

"Oh. Thanks."

"Well, you know. If I try to give them to her, her husband might not like it. I don't know if I can outfight him."

Maybe I wasn't his first choice for the flowers, but I loved them anyway and clung to them. "Thanks."

"Just a small way to say thanks for the bed, really. It's a lot more comfortable than the couch."

"Yeah. Sorry I didn't suggest it sooner."

"You didn't really know me, now did you?"

Hard to believe, because in a way it felt as if I'd known him forever.

We started walking back to the dorm, with the cart wheels squeaking.

"Do you have a girlfriend?"

"Nah. Who'd have me?"

I laughed so hard that the air rushed in, hurting my lungs. I wheezed, coughed. "Uh, any girl with eyes?"

He grinned. "Thanks for the confidence."

"No, seriously, have you never had a girlfriend?"

"I dated a girl for a while, but things didn't work out."

"Is that the reason you took this trip?"

"Nah. She was fun, but we were never serious. Our breakup was mutual. No harm, no foul. We had a good time, but it was never more than that."

I thought about that on the way back to the dorm. I'd had some good times with Rick. But that elusive something had been missing. I wondered exactly what the *more* was that Jude was talking about. And if I'd even recognize it if I had it.

I hadn't planned to spend the remainder of the afternoon cooking, but no one else was using the kitchen so we had it to ourselves. The dorm was eerily quiet. I wondered if anyone else was still here. Stephanie had headed home that morning. And I'd seen a couple of other people loading suitcases into cars.

Sitting at the island, Jude was wolfing down the brownies that he'd asked me to make as soon as we got back to the dorm. It was late afternoon and I was preparing the stroganoff while the potatoes were baking.

"I should have guessed that you'd be a dessert-first kind of guy," I teased.

He grinned. "Hey, why wait?"

He cut off a small piece of brownie and held it out to me—the way a groom would extend a piece of wedding cake to his bride. I leaned over and he shoved it into my mouth. Double chocolate was indeed very chocolatey and doubly delicious when it was shared with a guy.

"Are you going home at all over winter break?" Jude asked.

I stirred the stroganoff and took a quick peek in the oven to see how the rolls were browning. "No, actually. My parents are off touring in their travel trailer." I straightened and looked at him. "Have you ever traveled in a trailer?"

He shrugged. "No, but it seems like a lot of work."

"It is, but my mom doesn't like staying in hotels."

"She should try couch surfing."

I laughed. "She doesn't like staying in hotels because she doesn't know who's been sleeping in the bed. So I don't think she's a good candidate for couch surfing."

"How about you? You ever think about it?"

"I only just heard about it when Rick mentioned it a couple of weeks ago." I turned off the heat on the stove and oven. "Until I met you, I thought it was just a really bad idea."

"And now?"

I began setting the food on the table. "It's been fun having someone I didn't know stay with me, but"—I shook my head—"I don't know if I'd want to stay with someone I didn't know."

I placed a plate in front of him and in front of myself, before sitting at the island.

"Something smells good in here." Susan's voice.

I nearly jumped out of my skin as she pranced

into the kitchen. I had to quickly remind myself that having a guy in the dorm before lockdown was not against the rules. Still, I felt like someone attempting a prison break and suddenly having the search lights focused on her.

"Did you want some?" I asked, hoping she wouldn't notice Jude. Like that was going to happen.

"No thanks. It's like hours past lunch time and too early for dinner." She took a bottle of water out of the fridge, leaned against the counter, and zeroed her razor-sharp gaze on Jude. "I've seen you around here a couple of times."

When? How? Where? Was she peering out from behind curtains? I hadn't seen her when I was with Jude.

"I don't think we've met," she continued. "I'm Susan, the dorm monitor."

She stuck out her hand like a politician. Jude gave it a quick shake and I was hoping she didn't have any kind of psychic ability.

"Jude. Jude Hawkins," he said.

"That's not a Vermont accent you have there."

"Australian. Just in the area visiting. Lys

has been good enough to show me around."

A crease appeared between her brows. "Where are you staying?"

"With a friend."

I could see that she wanted to grill him further, but really what business was it of hers?

As though she came to the same conclusion, she said, "Well, enjoy your visit." She ambled out of the kitchen.

Thank goodness, because I'd been holding my breath and was getting dizzy.

"She seems nice enough," Jude said.

"I don't trust her. She is all about the rules. I'm surprised she didn't ask who your friend was." We might have to be a little more careful.

Jude dug into the stroganoff. "Not half bad."

I laughed. "What does that mean? Is that the same as not half good?"

He furrowed his brow like he was giving it serious thought. "To be honest, I never analyzed it."

"I'll take it as a compliment," I said, scooping up some potato.

"Absolutely a compliment."

My cell phone rang. It was a number I didn't recognize, a number with lots of digits. Had to be Australia. Ergo, it had to be Rick. I felt like my heart should have skipped a beat, that I should have felt a spurt of joy instead of . . . well, nothing actually, nothing more than *Oh, a friend. Wonder what he has to say*. I had this sudden recognition that our relationship had definitely flat-lined.

"You gonna answer it?" Jude asked.

"Oh yeah, sure." I swallowed. "Hello?"

"Hi, Alyssa."

There was as much excitement in his voice as there was in mine. Which was none. Either of us could have been saying, "Oh, look, chips in the pantry."

"How's Australia?" I asked.

"Way too awesome."

Could something be too awesome?

"What have you been doing?" I asked. He'd called me and I was the one working to get the conversation going. But that was how our conversations usually went. I led, Rick followed.

"Surfing, sunning on the beach. You know."

I didn't really, which was the reason I asked.

"Look, I called because I've been thinking about some stuff."

"What stuff?" I asked.

"You and me."

We were *stuff*? Okay, honestly that probably said more about the state of our relationship than anything.

"What were you thinking?" I prodded when the silence stretched between us.

He sighed. Since we'd been together I'd learned to read his sighs. They were like the "dude" commercials. Different inflections that said everything. He had the sweet sigh just before he kissed me. The hard sigh when we were studying together and he couldn't grasp the concept. The I'm-doing-this-for-you sigh when we went to the movies and saw a romantic comedy instead of blood, gore, and terror. And this one. The I-don't-really-want-to-say-this-so-can-you-read-my-mind? sigh.

Only, I didn't know what he wanted to say. I usually didn't. It was one of the reasons—right or wrong—that we'd decided to take a break.

"Rick?"

"I really like Marla. I think I might love her."

I hadn't been expecting that. Or the sadness that swamped me with the realization that in the time we'd been together neither of us had ever used the *L* word.

Had I only fallen in like with him and never in love? How did a person know?

"Wow," I said.

"Yeah. I know. But I'm feeling all weird about it."

"Why?" I said. The words seemed to be coming out of a tunnel. "We broke up."

"But we said we might—probably would—get back together."

I actually managed a soft kind of laugh, one that didn't sound as sad as I was feeling. "I'd say we're not going to do that."

He sighed. It was his sigh of relief. Like someone had just lifted a fifty-pound weight off his chest.

"Will you tell Marla?" he asked.

"What?"

"She didn't want to be the reason we broke

up. I tried to explain that we were taking a break, but . . . will you just tell her?"

Before I could say anything a girl was saying, "'Ello?"

"Marla?"

Jude's eyes went wide.

"Yeah," she said. "Are you Alyssa?"

She sounded nice, really nice. I didn't know why I was expecting someone harsh. She was Jude's sister, for goodness' sake. He was nice. It stood to reason she'd be too.

"Yes. Uh, Rick and I . . . we broke up. Before he left for Australia. It's totally over between us."

"Are you sure? Because he talks about you an awful lot."

Strong, silent Rick was talking an awful lot? That was hard to picture. Maybe he'd just needed the right girl to open up to. Maybe I hadn't been the one.

"I'm sure."

"I just don't want to be the other girl, if you know what I mean."

"I do. I absolutely do. Did you want to talk

to Jude? He's right here."

"Oh yeah, sure. Just a quick minute. If you don't mind."

She was paying for the call. Why would I care? Still it was nice of her to ask. I handed the phone to Jude. I tried really hard not to listen. I started carrying our dishes to the counter. Jude had cleaned his plate while I'd been talking to Rick.

Now I just needed to clean the kitchen. I'd made such a mess—of the kitchen, of my relationship with Rick, and maybe even my relationship with Jude.

I was standing at the sink, running water over the dishes before putting them in the dishwasher, when I felt Jude come up behind me. I hadn't even heard him say good-bye to his sister.

"You all right?" he asked.

I nodded, concentrating on the water washing over the dishes.

"You wanna talk?"

I shook my head. "Not yet."

I looked over my shoulder at him. "Deep

down, I didn't think we were going to get back together."

"But now you *know* you won't."

I nodded. "Yeah."

"You still want to go to the party?"

I forced a smile. "Absolutely."

Chapter 10

"Rick and I are not getting back together. Ever. He fell in love with someone else."

"You're kidding." Mel gasped.

We were in the kitchen of her house, putting little squares of cheese on crackers shaped like butterflies.

"Correction," I said. "He fell in love with *someone*. Not someone else. I'm not sure he was ever in love with me."

"Don't be stupid. Of course he was."

"No, Mel, he wasn't. And that's okay, because I wasn't in love with him either."

It was hard to admit that, but once I said it, I knew it was true. I released a sigh that sounded a lot like the weight-off-his-chest sigh that Rick had let loose that afternoon when we were talking.

Mel stared at me as though I'd totally lost my mind. "You guys were together the whole semester."

"Because it was convenient. We met. We lived in the same dorm. We were right there together. Same major. Same courses. Same exams to cram for. We liked each other, but honestly . . . there was no fire."

"What about Jude?"

I sat on a stool, put my elbow on the counter, my chin in my palm and snatched a square of cheese off a cracker. Mel immediately replaced it. I chewed thoughtfully. Something was definitely going on with us, but was I ready to admit that? I didn't think I was. "Convenience."

She shook her head. "No. No way. You're telling me you feel for Jude what you felt for Rick? Which it appears was pretty much nothing? I don't think so. You know what I think?" She snatched from my fingers the cheese I'd just snatched from the cracker, and put it back. "I think you're holding back, that's what I think."

"Holding back what?"

"Your heart. Your feelings. It's scary to put it out there. You said you thought the first guy you fell for would be *the one*. That's what you've been searching for. Like you think you'll meet him and a whole chorus of angels will sing and you'll know he's it! But it doesn't always work like that. Actually, I don't think it ever works like that. Usually you have to kiss a lot of frogs before you stop getting warts." She held up a finger. "Trust me. The Aussie is not a frog. You're not going to get warts."

"I could get hurt."

She lifted her arms and dropped them to her side. "Look, Boomer could come in here tomorrow and tell me it's over. I'm not what he wants. Once I smashed his family jewels with a good hard kick, I'd get over it. And when I wasn't mad at him anymore, I'd be glad for the time we did have together. The first time we kissed our braces got tangled up. He took me to the prom. He and I have been through a lot of firsts together, you know? He'll always be special even if it turns out that he's not with me forever."

"But don't you want him forever?"

"Yes, absolutely. But if it doesn't happen, I won't have regrets. Can you say the same if

Jude leaves and you never took a chance?"

I liked Jude a lot and that was scary. But she had a point.

"You came to the party with a hot Aussie. Why are you in here helping me put cheese on crackers?"

She'd handed Jude a beer when we walked in, and he'd taken it into the den to mingle with people and stand in front of the fireplace. I was only going to help Mel prepare some snacks before joining him.

"Because you apparently lack creativity when it comes to food and you aren't preparing anything more appetizing."

She shoved me on my shoulder. "Get out of here."

Jude was leaning against a wall, looking casual and sexy, watching a couple of guys bowling with their Wii. It was a small party, maybe a dozen people. Some people from work, some from the band. Others friends of Mel's I'd never met. Everyone was talking and laughing, cheering on the players, taking sides, then switching sides based on who was winning.

"Do you have one of those?" I asked, pointing to the Wii.

Jude handed me his beer. I took a sip, handed it back.

"Yeah," he said. "I already lost one tennis match to Boomer. I may be Wii'd out." He furrowed his brow. "So why did we have to wear bathing suits under our clothes?"

Mel had called and told me that they had something special planned. I knew what it was, but I wanted it to be a surprise for Jude.

"Guess we'll find out."

"Aren't you Miss Mysterious?"

Not usually, but tonight I was feeling good.

"Can't believe I didn't ask earlier. How was class?" Jude asked.

"It was fine. Nothing too exciting. I really should be studying."

He handed the beer back to me. "Don't think about it. Just relax."

Nodding, I took a couple more sips, finishing off the beer.

"Come on. I want to build a snowman," Jude said, taking my hand and leading me through the living room and into the kitchen. I threw the empty bottle into the trash can.

"I've heard that before. I think you want to build a snow*woman*."

"And this one won't be in a public park. We could have some fun with her."

He grabbed a bottle out of an ice chest, popped the top, and handed it to me. Then he reached in and got one for himself. He wrapped his hand around mine again and led me through the door leading outside. The porch light was on, illuminating the backyard, giving it a very Thomas Kinkade feel.

"Oh, look," Jude said, "a swing on the porch. Let's sit for a sec."

"Thought you wanted to build a snowman."

"Did I?"

"How many beers have you had?"

"Not many."

"That's not a number," I teased.

He dragged me over to the bench swing, sat, and pulled me down beside him. He lifted his arms to yawn, lowered one to the back of the swing, knocking the side of my head in the process.

"Smooth move, Aussie," I teased.

"God, I'm sorry." He tucked strands of my hair behind my ear. "You all right?"

"I'm fine. You didn't hit me that hard."

He moved in closer, pressed his head to mine. "That's not what I'm talking about."

I'd suspected that. He was referring to my earlier conversation with Rick. I'd been putting off talking about it with Jude. I didn't know why. I'd told Mel, but it just seemed more was at stake with Jude, that it might change things between us.

I sighed, deciding to just get this over with, like pulling a bandage off a scab.

"We broke up a couple of weeks ago. The reason was . . . how do I put this? Lack of enthusiasm? It was like we were just going through the motions. Today was just . . . I don't know. A final confirmation that it's over between us."

"Is it not what you wanted?"

I thought about that for a minute. "Actually, it was."

A heavy silence settled between us. He shifted his gaze away from me and drank his beer. I took another sip from mine and set it aside.

"With the girl you broke up with," I finally

said, "how did you know when it was over?"

He shook his head, still staring ahead. "I don't know. There were no scenes, no real breakup. We just looked at each other one day and said cheerio."

"Have you ever been in love?"

"I think so."

"Was it scary?"

"Not really, no. It was rather nice actually."

"But it wasn't the girl you broke up with?"

"No."

"Did you date her?"

"Not really. It was sort of a strange thing, a little complicated. I'm not sure she ever realized it, what I was feeling." He glanced back at me. "This thing with Rick, coming to a definite end. Shouldn't you be crying or something?"

"You'd think, but it seems that I have no tears to shed."

"How can I comfort you if you're not crying?"

"Did you want to comfort me?"

"Yeah. I really do." He set his beer aside and shifted slightly so he was at an angle that gave him a clearer view of me—and gave me one of him. He skimmed his fingers gently along my cheek. I was surprised they were so warm. "I want to kiss you, Lys. I've wanted to from the first moment I met you."

"What? When I pepper sprayed you?"

"All right. Maybe not from the first moment, but pretty soon afterward. Are you all right with that? Or do you need more time?"

I nodded. Shook my head. Answering first one question and then the other. Finally I decided I wasn't being clear. "I don't need more time."

"I want you to know it's not a pity kiss," he said very seriously.

"Okay." I hadn't thought it would be, but maybe after he left I'd wonder. My chest and heart tightened with that thought. I didn't want to think about him leaving, was wishing he wouldn't. He was only here for the winter break. Then he'd be gone and I'd never see him again.

He leaned in and kissed me. His mouth was warmer than his fingers, gentle. It was better than any kiss Rick had ever given me. I so didn't want to think about Rick. Not tonight. Not now. Maybe never again.

And then all I was thinking about was Jude. I felt his hand at my hip, then his arm came around me and he pulled me onto his lap without ever breaking away from the kiss.

Smooth move, Aussie, I thought.

I wound my arms around his neck, my fingers toying with the autumn-colored strands of his hair.

His kiss was tender and sweet. Everything that I needed at that precise moment. It seemed like he always knew exactly what I needed when I needed it.

"We've decided to initiate you into the polar bear club."

Boomer, Mel, and a couple of the party animals had come out onto the back porch and rudely interrupted what was turning into an incredible kissing session. Mel gave me an apologetic look. The others were smiling gleefully.

Horror swept over Jude's face as he connected

the dots. "Polar bear club? Isn't that where you jump into a freezing lake? No offense, mate, but you're mental if you think I'm going to do that."

"Don't be a wuss," I said.

Jude snapped his head around to stare at me. "You've done it?"

Truthfully, I'd have preferred to shoo everyone back inside and pick up where Jude and I had left off, but I knew these guys wouldn't go away until Jude had been dunked.

"Absolutely. I did it the night before I went home for Thanksgiving."

"But you grew up here. You're conditioned to the climate. You don't feel cold the way normal people do."

"Dude," Boomer said in a very disappointed tone. "You can't come to the cold climes and *not* join our polar bear club. You just can't, dude."

"Make me an honorary member."

"No can do, dude."

Jude groaned in surrender, throwing up his hands. "All right then. Guess I'm gonna do it."

We all got our coats and jackets before heading out.

"So where is this lake or river or wherever?" Jude asked.

"We use the university pool," Boomer said. "It's one of the few standing bodies of water that doesn't freeze around here. Zach's on the swim team. He has a key to the gym so he can practice over winter break."

"Oh, that doesn't sound too bad."

"Oh, it's bad," Boomer said.

"Then why do it?"

"Because it's bad."

"It's easier to get warm afterward when you're inside," Mel said, looking at me and rolling her eyes.

This little adventure was Boomer's way of having fun.

"But we need to be quiet going in," Zach said.

"My entire holiday is about being quiet," Jude said wryly.

"We'll go extreme sledding before the week is out," Boomer said. "You can yell all you want to out there."

"Extreme sledding?" Jude repeated, nudging his shoulder against mine.

"Can't explain it. You'll have to experience it."

"Okay," Zach whispered. "Everyone, quiet."

We were near the gym, standing behind some evergreens. The only people we needed to avoid were the campus cops who periodically patrolled. I suspected over the break they weren't as diligent.

Zach crept to the back door.

"Can't believe I'm actually going to dunk my body in freezing water," Jude said.

"You won't be alone. I mean, you'll go first, but then we'll all join you."

"You're all mad, certifiably insane."

Zach opened the door and made a waving hand motion. We all hurried inside.

We headed to the pool area. It was cool inside. They'd obviously turned the heating off. Zach switched on the pool lights. They created an eerie glow. I hoped Jude didn't notice the wisps of steam rising from the pool.

Boomer corralled him away from the pool. We all stripped down to our bathing suits.

"The easiest way," Boomer said, "is just to run and make a flying leap into the deep end."

He stepped back to give Jude room and it was my first glimpse of him without layered clothing to keep warm. He obviously did a lot of swimming along the coast of Australia. As a matter of fact, the other guys looked vampirish standing next to him. Jude was so bronzed. And so in shape.

He was jerking his hands, kicking his feet the way swimmers did standing on the block, waiting to take their marks.

He looked over at me. "I'm gonna do this."

I don't know what possessed me, but I stepped forward and took his hand. "I'll do it with you. And now that we're inside you can yell."

"All right. Let's do this. On the count of three. One. Two. Three."

We raced toward the pool, leaped off the ledge—he yelled, I laughed—and splashed into the chlorine depths.

He let go of my hand, his weight taking him farther down, so I surfaced first. He came up sputtering, surprise written all over his face.

"It's warm!"

"Well, yeah, dude." Boomer laughed. "Do you think we're all nuts?" He dove into the pool.

"This isn't a polar bear club," Jude said, and I heard the disappointment in his voice.

He was probably the only one among us disappointed when the initiation resulted in us landing in warm water.

"It's the *un*-polar bear club," I said. "Boomer's crazy joke."

"Oh, well. At least I got to see you in a bikini, which I certainly didn't think was going to happen in this kind of weather." He wiggled his eyebrows. "Nice, by the way."

"Back at you." Then I started swimming toward the shallow end of the pool.

Jude quickly caught up with me. I rolled over onto my back, paddling my feet.

"I was willing to jump into freezing water," he said. "Prepared to do it, actually."

"That counts."

"Don't think I can mark it off my list, though."

"Was joining a polar bear club on your list?"

"It would have been cool. But this will do until the real thing comes along."

We were at the shallow end and he stood up and pulled me to him, kissing me as the water lapped around us. I had this horrible thought that he was referring to us with his comment and not the club.

Please don't let him be talking about us, I thought wildly. Because for me at least, I was beginning to think it was the real thing.

Chapter 11

I sat in class the next morning, trying to focus on the lecture and not on thoughts of Jude.

When Boomer realized that Jude really wanted to be a polar bear, he'd offered to drive the two of them out to Lake Champlain for a quick dip and swim. It was so deep that it didn't freeze over. Jude had been majorly disappointed that I wasn't going.

But I needed to make it to class.

He'd had more success convincing me to skip class tomorrow to go extreme sledding. I'd never done that before—skip class. But I'd found someone to take notes for me. It was only one day and I'd make up the work later.

It was today that I didn't want to have to make up and if I didn't focus . . .

I looked more closely at my notes. Several

times I'd written "Jude Hawkins" and "Hot Aussie" in the margins of my notes. I was pathetic.

He'd slept in Sheli's bed again last night. Although he'd started in mine, just holding me close and kissing me until we finally had to say good night and get some sleep. Then he'd moved to the other bed.

Even though we weren't in the same bed, there was still a coziness to having him in the room.

I wondered if it was possible to really fall for someone as fast as I was falling for Jude. I wanted to do everything with him. I wanted to be with him constantly. I wanted—

"Miss Manning?"

I jerked back to the present and stared at my human genetics professor. "Sir?"

"I was asking your opinion on the material you were supposed to read for today."

Material I hadn't read because I'd been at a party. "Uh—"

"Mr. Karkosak?"

The guy two seats over rattled off his opinion as though it carried the weight of a

Supreme Court decision.

I never came to class unprepared. I'd just have to stay up later tonight to make up for tomorrow. Because for the first time in my life, I wanted to do something more than I wanted to study.

It was a new and invigorating experience, something I needed to explore.

Something I wanted to explore with Jude.

"Twenty-seven bottles of beer on the wall, twenty-seven bottles of beer . . . "

Seriously off-key voices filled Boomer's SUV as we headed to the Vermont back country for a little extreme sledding. Jude had started the song at a hundred bottles.

"Drink one down and wot 'ave you got? Twenty-six bottles of beer on the wall!" he shouted.

I was giggling, laughing so hard that I could barely sing his mutilated version of the song, because he always sang the last line of the refrain as though he was insulted that he couldn't drink beer legally in Vermont.

Mel was riding shotgun. Jude and I were

in the back. Jude was also proudly wearing a polar bear sweatshirt that he'd picked up in a gift shop the day before. He was an official member now, having actually swum in a freezing lake. On the car floor between us was a cooler filled with beer—for when we'd finished sledding.

"You can't drink and sled," Boomer had warned Jude. "Because, dude, extreme sledding is tight and you've got to stay focused, alert."

Extreme sledding—or free sledding, as it's also known—is extremely popular in Vermont since the sport began here several years ago. *World News Tonight* had even done a short feature on the sport. There were no established trails. Each sledder created his own, searching for the slopes that would give him the momentum he needed to sail through the air, doing stunts.

Boomer turned off the main road and followed a snow-covered trail. He pulled to a stop in what appeared to be an empty clearing. The nice thing about free sledding was that unlike skiing, it didn't require an actual resort, marked trails, or ski lifts. All we needed was a sled and a mountainous, forested area so we could trudge far up a hill and sled down. And Vermont was filled with mountainous, forested areas.

"Seems kinda warm out here after my experience yesterday," Jude said, rubbing his gloved hands together after climbing out of the vehicle.

"You're so proud of being a polar bear," I teased.

"Absolutely. Wish you could have been there."

"Maybe next time."

"I'm not doing that again. Once was enough, thank you very much."

Quite honestly, I was relieved, because jumping into icy water was not my idea of fun.

The day had turned gray, the promise of more snow hovering in the air. Visibility was still good, though. I figured at the closest resort some of the higher ski trails might be closed due to low visibility or high winds. But again, that was the beauty of extreme sledding. No one could shut us down.

As we gathered at the rear of the SUV, Boomer sprang open the back door.

I reached inside and grabbed my backpack, which I'd filled with protein bars and water.

The sport took a lot of energy and there were no little coffee shops around here. I took the radio Boomer gave me and shoved it in the front pocket of my pack.

Jude helped me slip my backpack on before snatching up his own. I could see the excitement in his eyes at the opportunity to try something new, something he'd probably never do in Australia.

"Here we go," Boomer said, handing me a Mad River Rocket, the official name of the sled.

"Looks like a baby bath fitted with knee pads on top," Jude said.

Boomer turned one over and ran his gloved hand along the runners on either side of a tunnel. "This creates a monorail as you're traveling down the slopes," he explained. "Helps you stay upright and it helps with the steering."

I put my hand on Jude's arm, wanting to reassure him. "Just remember that we all took tumbles in the beginning."

I dropped my sled to the ground, grabbed the tether, and started walking up the steep incline, Jude trudging along beside me.

"It's eerily quiet out here, isn't it?" he marveled.

I understood completely what he was talking about when he referred to the quiet. It was as though even nature was holding its breath. We were in the wilderness, away from any true semblance of civilization. Extreme sledding truly offered the opportunity to get away from it all.

"I love coming out here," I said reverently.

"You come often?"

"Not often, because of school, but I come whenever I can."

"You must enjoy it."

"Trust me. You're going to love it. I like it better than skiing."

Boomer and Mel, holding hands, hurried past us. "Come on, guys, let's hoof it. We've probably only got a few hours before that snow storm hits. Let's get this done."

A quick thrill shot through me when Jude's hand tightened around mine. He grinned at me. I grinned back. He wasn't the only one who was going to love being out here today. I was loving it already.

Something had definitely changed between us the night of the party. Even though I knew he was leaving, I'd convinced myself that I wanted to make the most of the time we had while he was here. I'd even given him his own blocks on my time chart.

We passed a scrap of red material tied to a bare branch.

"Boomer's leaving those rags, right?" Jude asked.

"Yes. To make it easier for us to find our way back to the car."

"This is a pretty isolated thing we're doing."

"We'll be fine. We've done it before. Just don't lose sight of me."

His grin broadened. "I'm not planning to do that."

And something in the way he said it made it sound like he wasn't talking about only today. I shoved those thoughts back. *Just take each moment as it comes.*

I peered over at him. His cheeks were ruddy and he hadn't shaved this morning. Insanely, I wanted to take off my gloves and rub my palms over his jaw, let the bristles tickle my skin. Or better yet, lean in for a kiss and feel them tickle my chin.

Suddenly Jude snaked his arm around me, tugged me up against his side, and spun us both in a circle until we landed behind a towering evergreen. My shriek mingled with laughter. The sound was cut off when he kissed me. Slowly. Thoroughly.

When he drew back, he said, "Sorry. My hundred-things list. Kiss a girl on a mountain. Had to, you know? Might never get another chance."

Smiling broadly—I didn't know if I'd ever smiled as much as I did when he was around—I teasingly slapped his shoulder. "You're telling me that when you wrote your list, of all the things to do in your life, you put *kiss a girl on a mountain*?"

"Well, no, not originally. Last night I scratched ride in the space shuttle off my list to make room for kissing a girl on a mountain. Seemed a greater probability of happening."

"You know, you probably could have gotten

the kiss without putting it on your list."

"Ah, well then, I'll put the space shuttle back in."

Then he lowered his head and kissed me again. I wrapped my arms around him and was tugging off a glove so I could thread my fingers through his hair when I heard, "Hey, guys!"

With a groan, Jude broke off the kiss and leaned to the side slightly, calling up the mountain, "Coming!"

He looked back at me. "I don't suppose we could just stay here and do some extreme kissing."

He had no idea how much that idea appealed to me and the sacrifice I was making. "You need to give the extreme sledding a try. You can do extreme kissing anytime."

"Really?"

Giving him nothing more than a sly grin, I grabbed his hand and started tugging him up the mountain.

Really, I thought. *Absolutely, positively, really.*

After an hour of hiking, we reached the top of our improvised trail. We were in the middle of nowhere. An expression I really never understood because obviously we were *somewhere*. On a mountain. High up on a mountain. With no cities, no buildings, nothing in sight except snow and trees and one another. The wind had picked up. Maybe because we were at a higher elevation. Thick, fat snowflakes had begun to fall. The sky had turned a dark gray, and the sun had gone into hiding, peering out from behind ominous-looking clouds every now and then as though it had suddenly become shy.

"We need to carb up," Boomer said.

Leaning against a tree, I dug into my backpack, pulled out a peanut butter protein bar, and handed it to Jude, then grabbed one for myself. Jude took a thermos of hot apple cider out of his, removed the top, and offered it to me. I drank, letting the warmth spill through me from the inside out—a feeling very similar to what I experienced when he kissed me. I gave the thermos back to him.

He put his arm around me. I smiled.

Click!

Mel was standing there with Jude's camera. She handed it back to him. When had he handed it off to her?

"Thanks," he said.

"No problem."

She walked off and Jude settled back in beside me.

"I really wish you'd give me a second to pose."

"I told you. I don't like poses. It's not the real person then."

"I think my mouth was open, like a bass or something."

"I doubt it. And even if it was, it would have been cute."

I couldn't win with this guy. Glancing around, I noticed something in the distant shrubbery. I turned back to Jude. He started to put his camera away and I grabbed his wrist. I rose up on my toes, leaned near, pointed toward the underbrush, and whispered low, "A snow-shoe rabbit."

Jude moved in closer to me as though he needed to do that in order to get a clearer look.

"Caw," he said, seeming truly intrigued. "You've got good eyes."

"It must have moved its nose or something

to catch my attention."

"Still, you're amazing."

His face was right next to mine and as I studied him, I wasn't certain he was even looking at the rabbit, wasn't certain he'd ever looked at it. I felt a tightness in my throat that I didn't understand. I wanted this moment to mean more than it should, more than it could. For all I knew maybe bagging an American chick was on his hundred-things list.

Keep it cool, Alyssa, I warned myself. I should heed my own advice, even when part of me thought it was stupid advice.

"Okay, guys," Boomer announced in that booming voice he had, the one that had probably earned him his name. "The wind's picking up so we probably need to start heading down. If you get too far behind, radio us."

While Jude was stowing away his thermos, I walked over to Mel. "Why is Boomer making such a big deal of the radios? We're not going to lose sight of each other."

She looked a little sheepish. "We may go off trail. You know, so you and Jude . . . "

She wiggled her eyebrows.

I groaned. "You don't have to make opportunities for us to be alone."

"Okay then. Maybe Boomer and I want to be alone. Besides, he takes this extreme sledding to new heights. He always heads for the more dangerous twists and turns. Honestly keeping up with us is probably not an option, so just enjoy a slow descent and don't worry if you lose sight of us."

"Okay." I glanced up at the sky. "Just don't get too far off trail. It looks like that storm is moving in earlier than the weatherman predicted."

"We'll be fine. Boomer is all about the outdoors."

"All right then." I turned to go.

"You like him, right? Jude?" she asked.

I stopped, glanced back at her. "Oh yeah. Big-time."

Mel and I walked over to where Jude was kneeling on his board while Boomer adjusted the strap over his calves. Jude sat back on his calves.

"Use your hands to move yourself forward," Boomer told him. "Once you get at a certain angle, your weight should carry you down. You use your arms to steer and to brake. Mel will go first so you can get an idea of how it works."

I set my board down beside Jude's, climbed on, and strapped myself in.

"You won't take off without me, will you?" he asked.

"Of course not. You're my partner."

Mel shoved off, hollering as her speed picked up. She took a turn and went between some trees. For a moment we lost sight of her, and then we saw her sailing over a snow bank, flying through the air, landing on the next slope with a yelled *whoop*!

"Got it?" Boomer asked Jude.

"Abso-bloody-lutely."

"Okay, show me."

He had a second to look panicked. "I didn't know I was going to have to perform for you."

"We all do the first time," I told him.

"Yeah, but I didn't get to see you."

"Okay, fine." I shoved off, traveling quickly down the incline a few feet. I used my body to angle the board, to slow my descent, and I came to a stop, looking back up the slope. I gave Jude a thumbs-up.

"Here I come!" Jude called out.

Then he shoved off and immediately tumbled over.

"It's okay!" I yelled up to him. "We all do that in the beginning."

Jude righted himself, smiling brightly. He shoved off again and traveled a little farther before eating snow again.

He pushed himself back up, got situated, then started off once more. He was barreling toward me. I tensed, preparing for impact—

Bam! Bumper sleds!

We were both laughing, tangled up together.

"We've got to stop meeting like this," he said, as we worked to untangle ourselves.

Boomer approached slowly on his sled. "I'll follow you if you want."

"That's all right, mate," Jude said. "I don't think it's going to take too long to get the hang of it. Worse comes to worst, I'll just walk down the hill."

"All right then." Boomer shoved off, heading down the slope. He detoured by a mound of snow that formed a natural ramp, went up and over, rocketing into the air and flipping over, before landing perfectly in the snow and continuing on.

"Ah, he's just showing off now, isn't he?" Jude asked.

I laughed. Yeah, Boomer had the moves down.

Mel rushed after him with nothing more than a quick hand wave back at us. She hit the same ramp, flying into the air and turning 360 degrees before landing.

Jude scoffed. "Think they're so good." He eyed me. "Do you have those kinds of moves?"

"Not those exactly, but I have the tumbling-head-first and the falling-over-onto-my-side moves pretty much down pat."

He narrowed his eyes at me. "You're just trying to make me feel better."

"No, seriously. I spend a good deal of my time just fighting to stay upright. But you'll master the simple moves before the day is over."

"You can go on if you want. No need to wait for me to catch up."

"No way. We're partners. Besides, I'm

pretty new at this too, so I don't travel as fast as they do. You'll probably go faster because you're heavier, so you go first."

"I think you just want to be behind me so you can watch me tumble."

I scooped up some snow and flung it at him, then I turned and headed down the hill.

"You're gonna be sorry!" he called after me.

I didn't think so. How could any girl be sorry when she had a hot Aussie on her tail?

Chapter 12

Jude overtook me with no problem. I preferred him in front because then I got to watch him skidding down the trail. I liked watching the way he moved. Just as I'd predicted, he'd caught on fast and was maneuvering himself toward natural ramps that could give him a more exciting ride.

We were having a grand time creating our own trails, skipping over little mounds of snow, making hairpin turns around trees, tumbling down rough slopes. Once Jude got the hang of free sledding, he was unstoppable and adventuresome. He was all about taking risks.

Traveling a short distance behind him, I watched as he hit a bump, went flying, hollering like a madman, then—

Splat!

I went around the lump in the snow and came to a controlled stop a short distance away from him.

"You okay?" I asked.

He shoved himself up, shook his head to clear it of snow, and rubbed his gloved hands down his face. "Yeah."

He looked over at me and grinned. "This is madness."

Chuckling low, I glanced off to the side and caught sight of something. I looked back and Jude already had his hands in the snow ready to shove off.

"Jude!" I whispered low, trying to get his attention without creating too much noise.

Luckily my voice carried because he glanced back. I unstrapped myself and got out of the sled, wobbled around a bit, forgetting how it took my legs a moment to adjust to the change. I motioned him over.

He unlatched himself, got up, and went straight down. I should have warned him about that. I staggered over to him and plopped down. "Give your legs a moment to adjust. There's something over there I want you to see."

My voice was tinged with excitement. I couldn't help it. I was hoping to have something special to show him. The tracks looked fresh. With the amount of snow that had begun to fall, if they weren't they would have been covered by now.

"What is it?" he asked.

"You'll see." *I hope.*

"Does it involve locking our lips together?"

"Maybe eventually."

"Then I'd better go for it now."

He put his hand behind my head and leaned in for a kiss. Maybe the tracks could wait.

Or maybe not.

I drew back. "Trust me, this will be awe-some."

Linking our arms together, we supported each other as we stood. Then we walked stiff-legged back to where I'd been, dragging the sleds behind us. When we got there, I took his hand and led him through the trees to what I'd spotted.

He knelt down, studied the indentation in

the snow, then craned his neck up to look at me. "What is it? A horse?"

"No."

"Cow?"

Smiling broadly, I shook my head and held out my hand. "You'll see. Let's follow the tracks."

He put his hand in mine and I pulled him to his feet, staggering back when he stood, lurching forward when he tugged me closer. I was breathing heavily as I landed against his chest. His arms came around me and for a second, staring into his green eyes, I forgot all about the tracks.

I gave myself a mental shake. "We don't have a lot of time because of the storm that's moving in, but you'll like this."

"How can I not if you're there?"

Okay, this guy had about a zillion ways to melt my heart. But I was strong. Instead of reaching up to kiss him again, I grabbed his hand and forced him to follow the tracks.

"We need to be really, really quiet," I whispered to him. "If this is what I think it is, we don't want to scare him off."

"How do you know it's a him?"

"Oh, well, I don't. I guess it could be a her."

We kept between the trees. Every now and then I caught a glimpse of a frozen lake in the distance. No one else was around and it was probably crazy to pursue.

But then I saw it and quickly crouched down behind a tree, drawing Jude down with me. It was a moose, standing alone at the edge of the lake.

"Crikey," he whispered in awe. "It's huge."

I was torn between being thrilled at his excitement over the find and teasing him about his reaction to it. I went with teasing.

"What? Are you the Crocodile Hunter's replacement?"

Shaking his head, he glanced over at me. "My mates and I, whenever we saw something interesting, we'd go 'Crikey!' and imitate Steve Irwin. He got so excited about things."

"I was so devastated when he died."

"It was freakish. I've swum around stingrays. They're gentle creatures. . . . What?"

He was no doubt reacting to my shocked expression.

"Don't do that anymore," I ordered.

He studied me for a minute, gave a little shrug—I didn't know if it was agreement or not—and looked back at the moose. "I thought they had antlers."

"Only the males. And they lose them in the fall. But come spring they'll grow back. You'd really say crikey then. They're massive. I wish you could see them."

"Maybe I'll make another trip over here."

I twisted my head to see him. His warm fingers touched my cheek and I wondered when he'd removed his gloves. He leaned in and gave me a quick kiss.

"I'm pretty sure I will," he said quietly. He glanced back at the moose. "Thanks for sharing this with me, Lys."

"Anytime."

We stood up and headed back to the trail. The snow was coming down harder, filling in the tracks we'd followed as well as the ones we'd made.

"Let's cut through here," Jude said.

I'd warned Mel about going too far off trail. I should have listened to my own advice.

"Any idea where we are?" Jude asked.

"Lost?" I squeaked, turning in a circle and seeing nothing except trees and snow-covered terrain.

"I was afraid of that."

The next obvious question was: Where were the others?

When Jude and I had emerged from the trees after spotting the moose, we weren't where we'd gone in, but we'd both agreed that as long as we headed downward, we'd eventually arrive at the spot where we'd started or we'd hit the road we'd come in on.

We were now as far down as we could go and there was . . .

Nothing.

No cars, no people, no buildings. Had we come down the wrong side of the mountain?

I'd forgotten to look for any familiar markers, for the red flags. *Stupid, stupid, stupid.*

Wind was whipping up the loose snow around us and icy sleet began pelting us.

I tried the radio and got the same thing I'd gotten the last six times I'd tried it: static. It made my teeth hurt, the sound as irritating as fingernails on a chalkboard.

"I just don't understand how this could have happened," I said.

"I do. I was spending more time watching you than keeping my eye on where we were going."

I suddenly grew so warm that I thought I was going to have to remove my jacket. I was surprised the snow around me didn't just melt and create a puddle.

"Because I'm so awesome on the board?" I asked.

Reaching out, he touched his gloved fingers to my cheek. "You're awesome, Lys. Absolutely."

I was certain that if we weren't lost he would have leaned in to kiss me. But right now we had to concentrate on survival.

He took a step back and glanced around quickly. "So what do we do now?" His voice held a seriousness that ratcheted up my worry level. If my fun-loving, life-is-to-be-lived-to-the-max Aussie wasn't grinning, we were in big trouble.

And when had I started to think of him as mine?

"Under normal circumstances I'd put on my problem-solver outfit and—"

He swung around. "What?"

He was looking at me as though I'd shifted into crazy-girl mode. Maybe I had.

"Bad joke." I shook my head. God, did I really want to take time to explain this? "When I read Rick's email to you, I had this vision of me in Superman tights with a big *P* for Problem-solver Girl on my chest."

He gave me his slow grin. Maybe it wasn't such a bad joke.

"So I'm about to discover that mild-mannered Lys is a superhero with a magic cape who can fly us out of here?"

"I wish."

His smile dimmed as much as the daylight had.

"You're scared," he said.

Didn't take a genius to figure that out.

"I'm terrified," I admitted.

He hooked his finger in my jacket and pulled me toward him. "It's gonna be all right."

He lowered his head and kissed me. In the frigid air, his mouth was so warm, and I thought if we could somehow harness that warmth we would be okay. The kiss was brief but it was enough to restore my confidence that we would survive.

"Well, we're certainly not going to make any progress by just standing here," Jude said. He pointed toward some trees. "I think we need to go that way."

I didn't have a better suggestion. "Agreed."

"So we'd best get going."

"Yeah. We should." I was nodding my head so fast that I looked like a bobble-head. "I have a flashlight."

I removed my backpack, knelt in the snow, unzipped it, and dug around until I found the flashlight.

"Don't turn it on until we have no choice," he advised. "Don't want to waste the battery."

"I've heard of people getting lost in the

wilderness for days and coming out alive," I told him.

"I don't think it's going to be as bad as all that." He took my hand. "Let's stay close."

I did my bobble-head imitation again, before falling into step beside him as he trudged toward the trees.

The snow thickened and the wind started howling by the time we reached the trees. I had visions of us trying to build shelter.

"You don't happen to have a pocketknife with you, do you?" I asked.

"Nope. Can't get them through security at the airport, didn't think to buy one when I arrived."

"Right."

"Why?"

"I was just thinking about shelter."

"I think we can use the sleds as a form of shelter," he offered. "Create a little tent with them."

"We'd have to scrunch up."

"I can scrunch."

"I guess if I have to get lost, getting lost with

an optimistic Aussie is the way to go."

The radio crackled to life and I nearly peed in my pants right then and there. "Hello? Ten-four over."

I don't know why I thought some code would strengthen the connection. It didn't. Another crackle sounded. Then nothing.

"Since we were able to pick up some sound do you think someone is near us?" I asked. "Are they trying to contact us?"

"Haven't a bloody clue."

"Do you think we should yell?"

"I guess we could give it a go."

"What do we say? Hello out there or—"

"How about help?"

"Yeah, that's the word we need."

We yelled in sync for a good five minutes, our hands cupped around our mouths, trying to increase the volume. We heard some twigs snapping, but decided it was just small animals scurrying away from the crazed sledders.

"Okay, let's move to plan B," Jude said.

He took my hand and we pushed forward—or at least I hoped it was forward. Who knew? We could be moving away from our group. How had this happened? Every time I heard some story on the news about people getting lost, I always wondered how they could be so stupid, so careless. And here I was. Stupid and careless and who knew what else?

Possibly dead.

Chapter 13

The farther we walked, the more trees surrounded us and hemmed us in. I was suddenly claustrophobic when I'd never been before. The bare, rattling branches seemed ominous, reminding me of skeletal fingers. The wind was screeching. It was as if we were extras in a really bad horror movie—the characters without last names, the characters who never survive.

Eventually the trees began to thin out and we found ourselves in another clearing as darkness was rapidly descending.

I squinted in the distance. "Is that a barn?"

"It's some sort of building."

"If there's a barn, there has to be a house." But even as I said it, even as I looked around for smoke coming out of a chimney, I saw nothing except that one building, all the snow, the trees, and the mountain waiting to be climbed.

"I say we go for it," Jude said. "If nothing else, it'll give us some protection against the wind until morning."

"Yeah," I said. "Good idea. Let's go for it."

All I really wanted to do was lie down and go to sleep, but somehow I managed to reach deep inside and pull up the gumption to move toward the barn. I pretended I was a puppet and someone was yanking my strings—foot up, foot down. Foot up. Foot down.

When I lost sight of the barn, I turned on the flashlight. There it was: a looming shadow in the encroaching darkness.

I thought we were going as fast as we could, but somehow we managed to quicken our pace, in spite of the fact that our feet were sinking into the deep snow. The sled was bumping along behind me, hitting my calves and threatening to trip me up.

We finally reached the barn. It didn't look nearly as sturdy close up as it had from a distance. As a matter of fact, I was fairly certain that a good strong wind would cause it to crumble like a house of cards. And a ferocious gale was circling around us. Was this really our last hope for shelter, for survival?

We took a slow walk around it. It had barely weathered the elements, and the boards were rotting, leaving gaping holes between some of them. I had a feeling we weren't going to find a house nearby in the morning. It was a deserted building, maybe a hundred years old. Wonderful. I always wondered where old barns went to die.

Jude pulled on the door. It creaked and groaned. When he had the door opened a crack, I picked up the sled and prepared to go through.

"Wait," Jude ordered. "Give me the flashlight. I want to take a quick look to make sure no dangerous animals are in there."

"I don't think anything big could get through the holes we've spotted. And since *we* had trouble getting the door open, I don't see how something—"

"I just want to check. Maybe it's been

living inside for centuries. Like the Loch Ness monster."

"I really don't like the idea of you going in alone."

"And I don't like the idea of you going in at all, until I've checked it out."

"You don't have to be heroic," I grumbled, handing him the flashlight. "Be careful."

He wrapped his arm around me, pulled me close, and dropped a mind-numbing kiss on my mouth. It was the kind of move I'd seen in movies.

He released me and grinned. "Just in case I don't come out."

Who did he think he was? Indiana Jones?

Before I could get after him for teasing me like that and scolding him for even thinking about not coming out, he'd disappeared through the narrow opening.

I crept up to it and peered inside, watching as Jude circled the flashlight around. My heart thudded with the thought of something being in there, some harm coming to him. I wouldn't leave him. I should have at least armed him with some snowballs.

There wasn't as much snow inside but it wasn't exactly warm and cozy looking, either. The good news was—no monsters.

"It's okay," Jude declared and walked back over, shouldering his way out.

We each picked up our sleds and went back inside. It actually didn't smell too bad. The cold weather had probably killed off any mold and frozen anything yucky. Here and there were piles of straw. It looked like the floor was just dirt.

A chill went through me that had nothing to do with the cold. The storm actually sounded much worse, much more ominous, inside the barn than it had outside. The wind screaming through the cracks sounded like demons rising up from hell.

"Here," Jude said, "you'll probably feel safer with the flashlight."

I took it from him, although the truth was that I felt safer with *him*.

"Shouldn't we close the door?" I asked when he didn't try to draw it back into place.

"I'm afraid if I do that we might not be able to get out in the morning."

"Good point." Although I thought a good hard kick would probably punch a hole in any of the outer walls.

I heard a scurrying sound and swung the flashlight wildly around. "What was that? Was that a mouse? Oh, God, don't tell me there are mice in here."

"All right, I won't."

I shone the flashlight on him. "You think there are?"

"They get cold too."

"How can you sound so calm?"

"They're just mice. Probably as afraid of us as you are of them."

"I'm not terrified of them. I just don't like them. So going to sleep tonight is completely out of the question."

"I don't think they'll bother us." He stomped his foot and then started kicking straw away. "Looks like there's just dirt beneath us. We could use the straw and what's left of some of the stalls to get a fire going."

"How? By rubbing two sticks together? I don't think that really works. Plus there's the challenge of finding two sticks."

He held up a lighter and flicked it. "Boomer and I had been talking about hanging around after we all met back at the car, building a fire, roasting marshmallows, and tossing back a few brews." A wistful look came over his face. "So, Superlighter Man to the rescue."

I laughed, quite proud of myself for not sounding too hysterical. "A fire would be great."

And would probably keep the rodents away.

"Just so you know, my costume will not involve tights," he said.

I squeezed his hand. I thought we were both putting on a brave front.

Jude found an old rusty pitchfork and used it to clear away an area in the center of the barn. We avoided going near corners and anything else that looked like nesting areas.

Snow sprinkled in through holes in the roof. It was magical really. Any other time I would have flung out my arms and twirled beneath it. Right now, though, I was having a difficult time appreciating the wonder of it.

Jude soon had a very small fire going. We sat on our sleds, watching the sparks shoot up and listening to the crackling of the straw and old wood. The heat felt heavenly after trudging so long in the cold.

"So I've done my part," Jude said. "What are you going to fix us to eat?"

"How sexist is that?" I teased.

"Pretty sexist, I'll admit. But I'm starving."

I set the flashlight aside, its beam of light shining toward a corner. Jude reached over and turned it off. The shadows crept in. Our small fire wasn't very good at keeping them at bay.

"We might need that later," he said.

"Okay, yeah." Naturally I hadn't brought any spare batteries. I put my backpack in my lap and unzipped it. "I have a couple more protein bars." I looked up at him. "Do you think we need to ration our food—just in case it's awhile before they find us?"

"They're gonna find us tomorrow."

"How can you be so sure?"

"We're gonna burn the building. Or at least take what we can outside and start a bonfire."

"That should get someone's attention."

"I hope so."

"Okay, then. One bar for you, one for me.

I've also got a few tiny boxes of raisins."

"I have some more apple cider. Don't know how warm it is." He pulled out a thermos.

I smiled. "We have a feast."

"It's gonna be all right, Lys."

Nodding, I pulled off my gloves and tucked them into my pockets for quick access. I couldn't tear off the wrapper with thick gloves on.

"I'll trade you," I said, holding out the opened protein bar.

I took a long, slow swallow, letting the now lukewarm apple cider do its thing and chase away the chills from the inside out. I handed the thermos back to Jude.

"I hope Boomer and Mel made it back to the car okay," I said.

"Now, see, I'm hoping they got lost so we won't look that stupid."

I laughed, not truly believing he was hoping they'd gotten lost. "You're not stupid. I am. I've done this before. I should have known better, should have paid more attention to where we were heading. I probably never should have gone off and followed those stupid moose tracks."

"Hey, it was worth it. It's a moment I'll never forget."

"I'm just glad we didn't have to work tonight."

"I think Paul would have understood."

"Actually, they might even call him to try to find us. He's a volunteer rescuer."

"I've always admired people like that—who help others."

"I just never thought I'd be one who needed to be helped." I felt incredibly silly. I had a feeling that I was going to have a hard time living this down—*living* being the key word there because as long as I lived through this I'd take all the teasing anyone wanted to dish out.

I took a bite of the protein bar and listened to the howling of the wind. At least I thought it was the wind. It stopped, then came again.

"Is that a wolf?" I whispered.

Jude stilled, listened. "Sounds like it."

"Do you think he can get in? Through the door? We should have closed the door." I eyed the nearby pitchfork. Would it stop a wolf?

"We'll be fine. It's a myth that they attack people."

"Is it?"

"I think so."

Still I scooted farther away from the door and nearer to Jude.

"Do you have wolves in Australia?"

"We have dingoes. Close enough."

I nodded. I thought I heard something snuffling around outside.

"What's your favorite movie?" I asked to take my mind off the predator which I was now envisioning slowly circling the barn.

"*Gladiator*."

"Because it stars Russell Crowe?"

"I might be a bit biased toward my fellow countryman, but no, I just like that era. The sword battles, the gladiators, the excitement, the adventure. It's not a romantic comedy."

"How can you not like romantic comedy?"

"Please. Silly girl meets silly boy. What's your favorite movie?"

"*Love, Actually*. Where a lot of silly girls meet a lot of silly boys and live happily ever after."

"Of course. Something romantic."

"Have you seen it?"

"No, but it sounds like a girl's movie."

"Which works since I'm a girl."

"That you are."

I heard appreciation in his voice, and I thought even without our fire, at that moment I'd have been warm.

"Favorite actor?" I asked.

"Have to go with Russell Crowe again."

"Favorite TV show?"

"You know, I don't watch a lot of TV."

"Really?"

"Really. What would you recommend?"

"I don't watch much either. Favorite book?"

"*I Am Legend*. Which, by the way, had a very different ending from the movie. The book's is far superior. What's your favorite book?"

"I haven't read for fun since the last Harry Potter came out. Pathetic, huh?" I sighed, planting my elbows on my thighs, and buried my face in my hands. "Oh, God, I'm losing two days here. I should be reading now. I have a midterm Friday and a paper due."

"They'll find us tomorrow."

I lifted my head and looked at him. "But no

way will they find us in time for me to get to class. So I've missed two class days plus my study time. I'm going to have to pull all-nighters—"

A *whoosh* suddenly echoed through the barn and a squeak sounded. I screeched, aware of movement, grabbed the pitchfork, and stood up, circling around.

There was no other sound, just an ominous silence. I didn't dare breathe.

Jude stood up and wrapped his arm around my shoulders. "It's all right."

My heart was thundering so hard that I was surprised it didn't start an avalanche somewhere. I clutched Jude's jacket. "What was that?"

The flashlight beam was suddenly shining along the rafters.

"There. An owl."

Larger than I thought an owl should be, it stared down at us with large dark eyes. It angled its head one way and then the other, studying us as if we were curiosities.

"It nearly gave me a heart attack." I sounded breathless.

"Good news is we're one mouse less."

I released a burst of laughter, almost a hysterical sound, and pressed my head against Jude's shoulder. "I love nature and the outdoors, but this is just a bit too close to the wild for me."

He pried the pitchfork from my hand.

"I'm not usually this jumpy," I said. "I'm a little embarrassed that I'm not being more brave."

"You're being very brave."

Kind words, but definitely not true. Together we sat on my sled. He put his arm around me and drew me close. I nestled my head into the nook of his shoulder.

"It's going to be a long night," I said, my voice low.

Jude pressed a kiss to the top of my head. "So if you could be anywhere right now, where would you be?"

I knew he was trying to distract me—just as I'd been trying to do with the earlier unimportant questions.

"Disney World maybe. All the scares there are fabricated. Nothing truly dangerous. How about you?"

"Quite honestly, as insane as it sounds, I

can't think of anywhere I'd rather be than right here."

He slipped his finger beneath my chin, tilted my face up, and kissed me.

Nothing was melting in this Vermont winter except my heart.

Chapter 14

Some time later, Jude found some dusty horse blankets that he shook out and piled on the dirt floor, giving us a little cushion to lie on. We both acknowledged that we weren't going to sleep, but made a pact to keep the other awake anyway, even if the conversation turned silly.

We were in the process of lying down when we heard a noise at the door. We both froze. A fox stuck its head inside, took a look around, and then retreated.

I let out the breath I'd been holding.

"I can't believe that only a few hours ago, I thought showing you a moose was going to be the high point of our animal sightings."

Chuckling, he stretched out and drew me in against his side, with me nearer to the fire. I welcomed the heat on my back. We unzipped our jackets and snuggled closer, absorbing each other's warmth.

"I bet this scenario never crossed your mind when you thought about traveling to Vermont," I said jokingly.

"What? Holding you close? I thought about it the first time I ever saw a photo of you."

I was trying to process that, unable to come up with a coherent response. The silence must have bothered him, because he said, "Why do you think I came to Vermont? I'm a sand and surf kinda guy. I'm used to feeling my toes at all times."

I shot up to my elbow and looked down on him. "*I'm* the reason you came to Vermont?"

"Yeah. I mean, at the time I didn't realize Rick was your boyfriend. I just thought you were friends, nothing more. You could have knocked me down with a snowflake the day you asked if I knew you were his girlfriend. I thought, 'Well, I've stepped in it now, haven't I?' Then you said you'd broken up and I had to fight not to grin like a fool with that news."

I remembered how stunned he'd looked. "Why would you want to meet me?"

"I liked your smile. In the photos Rick sent. Believe me, I know I sound bonkers."

"Do you do this often?"

"I've never done it before."

I didn't know how to respond. I was flattered and overwhelmed and maybe just a little terrified of what I was feeling for Jude. I'd never felt such intense emotions where a guy was concerned. He fascinated and charmed me.

I lowered myself back to his shoulder.

"Have you ever thought about moving to the States?" I asked, then cringed because I was trying to make this into something permanent. Why did I always have to think of a guy I was with as being *the one*?

"Yeah, I have, actually. Thought about getting a student visa, maybe working permanently over here. Have you ever thought about going to Australia?"

I laughed lightly. "Actually, I haven't thought about going anywhere. I mean, I've traveled in the States, with my parents in their trailer. As I got older, it became miserable. But other than that, I haven't been anywhere. I don't even have a passport."

"You don't have a passport? That's nuts!"

Sadly, I shook my head. "No passport."

"Oh, you've got to have a passport. What if you wake up one day and decide you just want to go somewhere? It takes weeks to get a passport processed. By then, the opportunity may have passed. You always want your passport ready to go."

"You're probably right."

"We'll go get you one as soon as we're rescued."

"What? No." I laughed. "I have to think about it. Have to get all the documentation together. And besides I'm not even sure I can fly."

Beneath my cheek, he went very still. "What do you mean you're not sure you can fly?"

"I've never been on a plane."

"Never?"

"Never."

"That's mental."

"No, we just never went anywhere that we couldn't drive to."

"You've got so much of the world to see."

I could hear in his voice that he was clearly baffled by my lack of adventure.

"I always thought I'd travel later, after college when I had a job and some money."

"Traveling doesn't take as much money as you'd think. You ought to get that passport. I might invite you to visit me in Oz, and then what?"

I felt my heart kick up at the thought. "Would you really invite me to visit you?"

"Yeah. I like you, Lys. I like you a lot."

"I like you too," I said very quietly. "Very much."

Silence settled between us—as though I'd made a grave confession. I listened to him breathing. Listened to my heart thrumming.

The wind picked up, shrieking through the cracks. The boards rattled. Somewhere something crashed. I cringed. Maybe the building would come down on top of us. The shadows danced in rhythm to the flames in our fire. The wolf's lonesome howl filled the night.

"Are you scared?" Jude asked.

"Yeah, actually, I am. I don't want to be. I want to believe that everything is going to be okay, I want—"

I felt him shift, his fingers touched my cheek.

"I meant are you scared about us."

I nodded.

"I'm scared too."

Then he gave me a lingering kiss. The wonder of it chased away all the fears, not only those we were facing tonight but the ones that I'd face when it came time for him to leave.

Jude drew back, tucked me into the nook of his shoulder, and pressed his large hand to the back of my head as though he was determined to keep me there. I could hear his heart pounding in rhythm to mine, heard him swallow.

The fears began to creep back in.

More than I wanted to be rescued, I wanted him to kiss me again.

"Lys? You awake?"

I couldn't believe it. I'd gone to sleep. In spite of my worries and all the creatures—

The creatures? Were they about to attack?

"What is it?" I asked, disgusted with the panic in my voice.

"Nothing. Listen."

I listened. I heard the owl hoot, but I didn't

think that's what he was talking about. It wasn't what I could hear . . . it was what I couldn't.

"The wind is gone."

"Yeah." I heard the marvel in his voice. "I think the storm is over. I can see some stars through the hole in the roof. Come on."

He sat up.

"Come on? Come where? It's still night."

"I know." He picked up the flashlight. "Let's go look at the stars."

He pulled me to my feet before I could object. Not that I had any arguments for not going.

I reached down and picked up the pitchfork.

He laughed. "What are you going to do with that?"

"It's the only weapon we have."

"All right."

He slid his arm around my waist, pulling me close, and we walked in tandem to the door, squeezing through. With the flashlight leading the way, we trudged through the snow for several yards.

When we stopped, Jude put his arms around

me, drawing me back in against his chest. "Ready?"

"For what?"

He switched off the flashlight.

It was as though the entire night sky suddenly opened up. It was so vast, the stars so bright. It was too magnificent for words.

"Look," Jude whispered. "A falling star. Do you see it?"

On such a clear night how could I not? I nodded.

"Quick, make a wish," he said.

I closed my eyes, leaned back into him, and wished tonight would never end.

Sometime after our trek outside, once we got settled on our makeshift bed, we both managed to fall asleep. We also shifted around. I awoke to find Jude curled around me, my back to his chest, one of his arms serving as a pillow for my head, while the other held me close. It was probably the most romantic way I'd ever been held, certainly the most romantic way I'd ever slept.

I opened my eyes. Sunlight, instead of snow,

was spilling in through the cracks.

"We survived," Jude said from behind me.

I guess something had alerted him to the fact that I was awake.

"We did."

"So I guess we need to start our signal fire," he said.

"Yeah."

But neither of us moved.

I felt him touch his lips to the back of my neck. "I know it sounds crazy, but I'm going to miss all this."

"Me too."

"But the world beyond this barn awaits."

"I hope so."

Jude rolled away from me and groaned low. I jerked around. "What's wrong?"

"My arm fell asleep. And it's cold! I let the fire go out." He was rubbing his arm.

I zipped my jacket, because our cocoon of warmth had dissipated quickly. Then I reached over and zipped his while he rubbed his arm.

"I've got some chocolate-covered mints," I said, scrounging around in my backpack and pulling out the little box. "I believe chocolate is essential to survival. I never travel without it." I poured some of the mints into his open palm.

He wolfed them down. Normally I savored anything chocolate, but I was hungry too, and I ate them just as greedily.

Then I tried the radio again. Nothing but static. I tried my cell phone. No signal.

"All right," Jude said, getting to his feet. "Let's get rescued."

The clearing was large enough that I didn't think we were in danger of setting the entire forest on fire. Jude was able to easily pull off more boards from the stalls and haul them outside to create our little bonfire.

The fire was larger than the one we had in the barn; the warmth was welcomed. We sat on our sleds and waited.

A lot of tracks were circling the barn. I pointed toward a set. "Do you think the wolf or fox made those?"

"They're small. I'd say the fox."

"And those."

"The wolf."

I released a deep breath. "Glad I didn't see those last night."

"But I was right. Nothing attacked us."

"Still, I wouldn't want to tempt fate with another night out here. How long do you think we should wait before trying to find our way to civilization?"

"Maybe give it until midday, then we'll see."

What struck me about Jude was that he never complained; he was ever hopeful. We would get rescued. We would survive. Everything would be all right, and we would add our latest adventure to the things we'd laugh about years from now.

"If I had to get lost in the woods, I'm glad it was with you," I finally told him.

"Wish I knew more about surviving under these conditions."

"I think you're doing a terrific job."

He gave me a look that said he appreciated the sentiment, but I was bonkers.

Then I heard it.

Thwup. Thwup. Thwup.

I looked up at the clear sky—and there it

was! A rescue helicopter.

I released a scream, jumped up, and started waving my arms frantically, and Jude started doing the same.

The helicopter began to descend.

I spun around to face Jude and released another scream. This one resonated with joy.

"We're rescued!" I shouted over the increasing noise of the whirring blades.

"Abso-bloody-lutely!" he cried.

Then he picked me up, twirled me around, and planted a kiss on my mouth that made me dizzy.

"We're fine, Mom, absolutely fine. You don't need to turn the trailer around and head back up here."

I'd called my mom as soon as my cell phone reception had returned. They were listed on my employee application as emergency contacts so Paul had called them as soon as he was notified that we were missing. Further attempts to turn my mother's hair gray were made when the rescue efforts made the national news.

How embarrassing was that? To have our

idiocy nationally televised. Obviously it was a slow news day if we were what the media chose to report.

To make matters worse, I, who did not like candid shots, had a news camera and microphone shoved into my face when the helicopter touched down at the ski lodge that had served as the command center for the search and rescue team.

"How in the world did you get lost?" Mom asked.

I sighed. "I don't know. We weren't paying attention and the storm came in . . . I mean, even the newscasters talked about the poor visibility."

"But you know to be careful, Alyssa."

Yeah, but I was also distracted by a hot guy. Not that I was going to confess that to my mother.

"Don't scold her, Renee. She could have died out there."

They had the speaker phone on so they could both hear me and I could hear them.

"Baby, we were worried," my dad said.

"I know, Dad, I'm sorry. You really didn't

need to worry. It wasn't nearly as bad as the news reported."

I had no idea what the news had reported, but I was sure it was exaggerated.

"Who is this guy you were with?"

How did I even explain what he was? Did I even know? Was I afraid to face it?

"Just a friend."

Jude was standing nearby, a blanket provided by the rescue team draped around him. Something passed over his eyes before he looked away. What was that look? What did it mean? And why had I felt an overwhelming need to put such a simple label on what wasn't at all simple?

"Is he okay?" Dad asked.

"We're both okay. Please don't turn the trailer around," I repeated. I wasn't up to dealing with their hovering over me.

And they would hover. They always did. Quite honestly, I thought my going away to school had been good for them. Before, they never would have taken a trip without me.

Maybe we were all stretching our wings.

"Are you sure? Because we're close to an

airport now. We can leave the trailer—"

"I'm sure." They'd probably started driving as soon as Paul called.

"Give your mother a call tonight before you go to bed."

"Okay."

"As a matter of fact, call her every night before you go to bed. She worries."

And he didn't? Get real.

"Okay, Dad."

After a couple of rounds of love-yous, be-carefuls, and see-you-soons, we finally hung up.

I couldn't wait for life to return to normal.

"How did you get lost?" Mel asked.

I was really getting tired of that question. Maybe we should have held a press conference instead of just saying that we were fine and heading away from the press.

We were at a restaurant at the lodge where the chopper had landed, eating breakfast—*eating* being a loose term for how we were wolfing down the food. My mother would be appalled by my table manners, but I'd never been so hungry in my entire life.

Boomer and Mel had taken a room for the night so they'd be around to help with the search. The lodge gave Jude and me each a room so we could shower. They also provided us with complimentary lodge logo sweats.

Paul was there. He'd been in the chopper and had checked our vitals. I'd never hugged him before, but I had at that moment. If I could have gotten to the helicopter pilot, I would have hugged him, too. Everyone was my hero that morning.

As the chopper carried us toward the lodge, it had been a little embarrassing to realize we were only a few miles away from it. We would have eventually run into it, if we'd just kept going in the direction Jude had suggested.

"I don't know how we managed to get lost," I said, pouring maple syrup over my second stack of waffles. "It seems silly now, but our sense of direction just got all screwed up, I guess."

"Hey, look, you're famous," Boomer said.

I glanced over at the TV hanging in the corner. People were coming off the rescue helicopter. Jude looked calm and collected, smiling and nodding at the reporters. Beside him was a girl whose black hair was sticking out all over the place. Dirt covered her face, and her huge, wide-open eyes were screaming, "I'm a psycho!"

Where had she come from?

"Omigod! That's me!"

Thanks a lot, FOX News!

Couldn't they have waited until we'd cleaned up?

"Please, don't let my mother see that." I groaned.

A reporter—of course it would be a very beautiful and put-together woman—put her microphone and her bright smile in front of Jude. "What can you tell us about your ordeal?"

He gave her his killer grin. "We survived."

"How did you manage that, facing last night's winter storm?"

"We found shelter in a barn. I probably owe somebody for the wood we burned."

The reporter laughed. I thought if the camera wasn't on her, she might have pinched his cheek.

"How did it feel to get rescued this morning?"

"Bloody marvelous."

She shoved the microphone into my face. "Did you have any doubts that you would be rescued?"

"No," psycho-girl trilled.

Then the reporter moved back to speak into the camera, but she didn't have anything to say that I wanted to hear.

"I don't even remember her asking me a question."

"You could have used a little makeup," Mel said.

I glared at her.

She held up her hands. "Sorry, I'm just saying."

"And what was that, how did you feel about getting rescued? How did she think we felt?"

"I think they're just looking for questions with simple answers for their sound bites," Jude said.

"How did you manage to look so good, and I looked like . . . crap?"

"You did not. You looked like a survivor."

A survivor who wanted to weep. I really needed some political scandal to come up that would reduce my air time.

"While we're here at the lodge, are we going to ski?" Mel asked.

Just the thought of more activity wore me out.

"You're nuts, you know that?" Boomer said fondly. "I'm ready to get home."

At the same time, Jude and I both said, "Me too."

When we got back to the dorm, Jude crashed on Sheli's bed.

I had some major catching up to do on schoolwork. Paul had given us the night off to recover from "the ordeal"—thank you thank you thank you. So I had an unexpected block of time to study, and did I ever need it.

I'd emailed a couple of students I knew and gotten notes from the classes I'd missed.

I was sitting at my desk reading some of the material the professor had posted for my human genetics course—the one with a midterm waiting for me in less than twenty-four hours.

The problem was that my gaze kept drifting over to Jude stretched out, facedown on the bed with the pillow over his head. He was still in the lodge sweats, but I found him irresistible.

What baffled me was that I was never distracted when I'd been studying with Rick. Never.

And all Jude was doing was sleeping. He didn't even snore. He didn't twitch. He wasn't restless. He was dead to the world, but so not dead to me. I just couldn't stop looking at him, couldn't stop wanting to walk over there and curl around him. Hold him, let him hold me.

What was this madness?

Was it survivor's infatuation? Was it some sort of mental disorder?

I don't know how long I studied him instead of my notes. But I noticed a subtle shifting in his body, like a long, lazy stretch. A hand came up and tossed the pillow aside. Slowly he rolled into a sitting position and yawned. He grinned at me. "G'day."

"More like g'night."

"Really?"

He looked at the window. It was dark outside. Almost dark in here. Only the lamp at my desk was casting out light.

"I can't believe I slept that long."

He got up and sauntered over to the desk. "So, how 'bout I ring up Boomer and see if he and Mel want to meet us at that club? We could get a bite to eat—"

"I can't."

He raised a brow. "You can't eat?"

"I can't go out."

"Well, then we could call in a pizza, right?"

"No, I can't do anything with you. I've got a midterm to study for and"—I picked up a paper and tossed it down—"a research paper to write."

Jude turned the paper around. "'Sexuality in the Victorian Age.' I thought they were all repressed back then."

"I guess I'll find out if I can ever get to the library to research those sources the professor listed."

"We could—"

I cut him off before he could make any other suggestions. "No, my number one priority is studying for the exam. Do you know how much time I've lost this week?" I picked up my time schedule, the dry-erase board that gave me two weeks at a glance. "I'm hours behind."

"But if you took a break, came back refreshed—"

"No, Jude. I can't." I pressed my hands to my head. "What was Rick thinking when he sent you that email? He knew I was going to be studying and wouldn't have time to take care of problems." I knew I sounded a little mean, but I was so stressed out I couldn't help it. I sighed, gave Jude a wry smile. "Go have fun."

I wrote down my cell phone number. "Call me when you need to get back in."

"Yeah, all right. I didn't mean to be a bother."

Oh, it hurt my heart when he said that.

"You're not. It's me, not you." I groaned. "I can't believe I just said that."

I got up, went around the desk, and hugged him. "Tonight I need to do this. So just have a good time."

"Right. What time are you going to bed? I don't want to wake you."

"Don't even worry about it. I'll be up all night."

When he left, I felt this strange urge to cry. Maybe it was an accumulation of the past few days, getting lost in the woods, knowing that my perfect G.P.A. was on the line. I couldn't goof off at all if I wanted to go to med school.

Jude had made me forget, and as lovely as it had been, now reality was about to bite me on the butt.

Jude didn't stay gone long. Maybe an hour tops. He brought back a bucket of chicken and insisted that I eat.

"No one can study with an empty stomach," he'd said.

He had a point. I'd decided that I could allot twenty minutes to wolfing down chicken that would probably clog my arteries.

But the twenty turned into an hour as I listened to him telling me stories about his mates back home. I thought maybe he was feeling a little homesick. Or maybe I was.

"I've gotta get back in there," I said finally, unfolding myself off the couch.

"Is there something I can do to help?"

"Nope. No one can study for me except me. I'll get it done." I took a step toward the bedroom and stopped. "I won't be able to do this next week. Play with you, I mean."

"All study and no play will make Lys a dull girl," he teased.

I wanted to tease back. Instead I said somberly, "Then I'll have to be a dull girl."

Chapter 15

I walked out of the classroom with an immense sense of relief. It only intensified when I saw Jude leaning against the wall.

Grinning, he shoved himself away from the tile. It was then that I noticed the bouquet of flowers. If hearts could weep with joy, mine would have.

I quickened my pace and met him halfway. Students were making their way around us, some staring as they went by, but I didn't care.

"How do you think you did?" he asked.

Almost giddy, I smiled brightly and nodded. "All right. I think I aced it. My four-point-oh is safe."

"That's great. Absolutely great." He held out the flowers. "These are for you."

I took them from him, smelled the roses.

"You shouldn't have."

"It was the least I could do after all you've done for me when you had all this on your mind. I'm really sorry."

"No, it's all right."

"No, it's not. I wanted to tell you in person."

Someone knocked my shoulder in passing. Jude scowled, took my arm, and led me over to the windows that overlooked the campus.

"Anyway, I wanted to let you know that I'm not going to be in your way anymore. I found another place to crash."

I fought to hang on to my smile, not to reveal the devastation I was feeling with those few words. "Oh."

"With a bed actually. At Boomer's. Don't know why I didn't think to ask him sooner. It makes sense. He's got an apartment. Look." He reached into his pocket and pulled out a key as though it was a ticket to the premiere of a Russell Crowe movie. "I can come and go as I please. It's perfect."

I swallowed hard. Or I would have if I had

any saliva, but my mouth had gone dry. So I just nodded.

"You've got what? Five more days of classes?" he asked.

I nodded again, and realized that I'd lost the smile.

"So maybe when you're finished we can go out for a pint, well, not beer, of course, but you know—Coke, Dr Pepper, water, whatever you want."

"That . . . that'd be nice."

"And I'll see you at work."

I shook my head. "Well, not tonight. I asked for the night off. I have to get that paper written. She's extended the due date until tomorrow at six A.M."

"Well, good luck with it. I have no doubt you'll blow her away." He leaned in and kissed my cheek. "I'll see you around."

He walked away then.

And I let him go.

All the way back to the dorm, I kept telling myself that everything had worked out for the best. I could get my paper written without any interruptions. I could get back on my study track. I could get back on schedule.

And the decision was a no-brainer for Jude. With the key he had independence. He didn't have to sneak around like an unwanted guest.

But the suite seemed so quiet when I walked into it. Somehow diminished. Boring.

I screwed the top off a wide-mouthed water bottle and put the flowers in there. I really needed to get a proper vase.

I grabbed a bag of chips, one of the remaining ones Jude had bought, and wondered vaguely why he hadn't taken them with him. He should have. He paid for them.

I was barely thinking, couldn't make sense of things. I needed to get focused. I had that stupid paper to write. I'd blocked out the rest of this afternoon and all of tonight, right up until dawn for putting together an amazing research paper. But first I had to get to the library to pull those sources.

I should have stopped on my way back to the dorm. I groaned. When had I become such a poor planner, wasting time I didn't have to waste?

I'd do some Internet research while loading up on chips. Then I'd head out. I went into my bedroom, worked my way out of my coat—never releasing my hold on the chips—and tossed it on the bed. Then I walked to my desk and stopped.

There was a stack of papers on it that hadn't been there when I left that morning. On top was a note:

Hope this helps make up for the time you lost.
—J

I ruffled through the pages. They were copies of the documents that I'd needed to research for my paper. At least four hours worth of gathered data, printed and neatly stacked on my desk. All I had to do was read it. I didn't have to look it up.

While I had been in class, while I'd been taking a midterm, Jude must have been in the library. But if he left here, how did he get back in?

Then I noticed something else that Jude had left. A framed picture of Jude and me.

Based on the background—snowy mountains and trees—it was the picture Mel had taken the day we went extreme sledding, just before we headed down the mountain. I was smiling. I looked happy and carefree. And Jude . . . he looked as hot as ever, his g'day grin broad, his arm around me, his cheek against mine.

Did I really think that what I had with him came anywhere close to what I'd had with Rick? What I had with Jude was so much *more*. With him I had the *something* that both Rick and I had been looking for. I knew then that Rick had found it with Marla.

I was glad for him.

I thought about blowing off the paper, but I couldn't. Not after Jude had sacrificed his morning to gather the materials I needed to research.

But I did need to get one burning question answered before I could focus.

I went downstairs to Susan's room and knocked on her door.

"Oh, hey," she said, when she answered. "I saw you on the news—"

Great.

"—and meant to check on you yesterday, but I figured you were recovering and preferred quiet. That whole ordeal must have been awful."

I shook my head. "Actually it wasn't too bad."

"Still." She left it at that and shuddered.

"I was wondering. Did you let someone into my room?"

"Yeah. That Aussie? He said he'd stopped by yesterday afternoon to visit you and left his duffel bag." She shrugged.

"Thanks."

"He's the one you got lost with, right?"

"Yeah."

She gave me this wicked little grin that looked so un-Susan I figured I was suffering some sort of aftershock.

"He is hot. I'll admit that I wouldn't mind getting stranded with him."

"I'll see you." I turned to go.

"Is everything okay? With your room, I mean. He asked to leave something in your bedroom. Just looked like some papers."

"Yeah, everything is great."

Or at least I was hoping it would be when I finished writing the damn research paper and had a chance to talk with Jude.

A few hours later, with my research paper finished in record time and emailed to my professor, I leaned over my desk to free up some blocks on my time chart—and then decided, no, my time-blocking days were over.

After a hot shower to loosen up my neck and shoulders, I carefully applied a little more makeup than usual. Not that I thought Jude really noticed makeup, but since he'd been here, we'd been all about the snow and just hanging out. I really hadn't done anything to make myself look more attractive, but tonight I felt a need to pretty up. Maybe it was because of the off-helicopter interview.

I brushed my hair a hundred times so it really shined and I left it loose to swing over my shoulders.

I couldn't remember the last time I'd worn a skirt. A wedding maybe. But I put on wool tights and a knee-length red skirt and sweater. I pulled out heeled black boots. I was placing my ankles in jeopardy by wearing them, but I wanted to look sexy. Just once, I wanted him to see me in something that wasn't thick, bulky, and designed to keep me warm. Or something that looked the same on a girl as it did on a guy.

Of course, the parka ruined the whole effect, but it was coming off as soon as I walked through the restaurant doors.

It was eight thirty when I burst through the back door of the restaurant. I hung my coat on the rack before making my way into the kitchen.

"Hey," Mel said. "Didn't expect to see you tonight." She gave me a once-over. "Don't you look good."

"Thanks." I glanced around. "Is Jude—"

"He's waiting tables tonight. Your section."

That surprised me. Paul put waiters through this whole training program. But Jude's waiting tables worked for my plan.

"Well, then, maybe I'll order dinner tonight."

"I guess you know he's staying with Boomer."

"Yeah. I actually want to talk to him about

that." It was warm in the kitchen and my face was starting to perspire. Not the look I wanted. "I'm just going to pop into the dining room."

And immediately wished I hadn't when I spotted Jude crouched at Hailey's table. He was smiling broadly and talking to her as though he thoroughly enjoyed her. Hailey was alone, not with her family, and I had a feeling she'd come with a specific purpose in mind—a purpose that went by the name of Jude Hawkins.

"Don't let it get to you," Mel said in a low voice from behind me. "He charms everyone like that. It's the reason Paul moved him to waiter. People order more food."

"You don't have to explain it. I know how charming he can be. I just thought—"

He looked up and caught my gaze. He looked surprised and, if I was reading his expression right, guilty. Slowly he unfolded his tall, slender body.

"You know what?" I said quickly. "I've changed my mind about eating here. I'm really craving McDonald's."

"Alyssa—"

Whatever else Mel was going to say was

lost because I was already through the swinging kitchen door and headed for the back one. I grabbed my coat, but didn't even bother to put it on before dashing outside.

As I crossed the parking lot, I almost slipped in the stupid heeled boots. What had I been thinking putting them on?

I leaned against a car, unzipped the boots, and jerked them off. Yes, I'd probably get frostbite but that was better than a broken ankle. Then I sprinted back to the dorm, tears crystallizing on my eyelashes.

It was better to just concentrate on my studies. No broken hearts there.

I was decked out in my finest flannel pajamas and thick woolen socks. Still eating chips. I'd gone through three bags now, having never stopped anywhere for dinner. I was also, much to my disbelief, watching *The Holiday,* which wasn't half bad. I could really relate to the main characters. Of course every time Jude Law made an appearance, I'd think of Jude and get distracted remembering all the reasons I'd fallen for him. I probably should have gone with another movie, but misery loves company and all that. I didn't think anything could make me more miserable than I already was.

I was sitting on the couch wrapped up in the comforter that had kept Jude warm for so many nights. Every now and then I thought I could smell him.

I'd had a nice long talk with myself when I got back to the dorm, similar to the Stephanie method of asking and answering questions posed to myself. The very idea of getting seriously involved with Jude was nuts. He was only going to be here for a couple more weeks. Then he'd go back to Australia and I'd probably never see him again.

Rick and I were over and that was good too. All I had in my life now was schoolwork and my job at the restaurant, a combination that would create no distractions once Jude had gone. I might even add another course in the spring. I'd seen a special on the news about a guy who had finished college in a year. Maybe I could shoot for two.

I heard the branches of the tree outside my room suddenly scratching against my window.

It had been so clear when I'd run home that I was surprised a winter storm was coming in. But they were so unpredictable. That was the reason Jude and I had ended up spending a night in a barn. I didn't want to think about that night, about how close I'd felt to him. Against all odds, it had turned out to be the best night of my life.

Then I heard some tapping against the glass in my room. Hail? Sleet?

Did it matter?

But why was it just hitting my window? Since our suite was on the top floor, when we had rough weather, I usually heard the patter on the roof. Strange.

The wailing of the wind caught my attention. It sounded isolated, as though it was just coming from my bedroom.

I muted the TV.

Was the wind calling my name?

I got up, walked into my room, and nearly had a heart attack on the spot. I hurried across the room to the window and yanked it open.

"Are you nuts?" I yelled at Jude. "How long have you been out there?"

"Just move. I'm coming in."

He leaped across and barely got his head in before he lost momentum. I shrieked and grabbed him. His feet were scrabbling against the wall.

"Come on, come on."

With a grunt, I gave a hard yank and pulled him in. He landed on the floor with a thud. I closed the window and crouched down.

"Are you okay?"

He nodded. "Just need a minute to thaw."

I touched his hands. They were like ice.

I ran into the bathroom, turned on the hot water, and began soaking some hand towels. I carried them into my room and wrapped them around Jude's hands and feet.

"Ah, lovely," he said, stretching out on his back.

"What were you thinking?" I asked.

"That I needed to talk with you and you weren't answering your phone." He gave me a pointed look. "Did you finish your research paper?"

"Yeah, I did. Thanks to you. Pulling all

those sources really helped to speed things along. Thanks."

"Least I could do." He pushed himself to a sitting position and leaned against the wall.

A few hours ago I'd thought I'd never again see him in my suite.

"I saw you in the restaurant," he said. "Why'd you run off?"

I shrugged, feeling silly. "I don't know. I was just going to thank you for your help with the paper, but you were busy. Everyone was busy. Wow. You really had a crowd—"

"Lys?"

I stopped my incessant babbling.

"You got all dressed up like that just to say, 'Thanks, mate'?"

I felt so awkward. I'd always thought Rick was the one not communicating, but here I was not willing to reveal what I was feeling, what I was thinking.

"I had some empty blocks on my time grid, so I thought when you got off from work, we could go grab a pint or Coke or whatever." I shrugged. "I wanted to look nice."

"You did. You looked very nice from where I was standing. Wouldn't have minded seeing you close up."

He made me want to smile, but I'd made such a fool of myself.

"I saw you with Hailey."

"I told you I don't like her, but she's a customer, so I can't be rude to her, now can I? Plus she leaves a generous tip and everyone gets a piece of that, so I was just helping my mates out."

I didn't know what to say to that. He was right, of course. About so much. But not everything.

"How are your hands and feet now?"

"Better I think." He removed the towels. "Want to move to the couch? It's a bit more comfortable than the floor."

"Okay, sure."

I put the towels in the bathroom and joined Jude in the living room. He'd removed his coat and was sitting on the couch. He was wearing a black cable-knit sweater and black jeans, so I knew he'd gone to Boomer's and changed after work. Did he want to impress me now like I'd wanted to impress him earlier?

"What are you watching?" he asked.

"Something silly." I sat down on the couch and pulled my legs up beneath me. I looked at him, then looked away.

"You can watch it if you want. I don't mind," he said.

I picked up the remote and hit PLAY, then hit STOP.

"It wasn't lost time," I said.

"What?"

I forced myself to meet his gaze. "On your note. You said it was to help make up for the time I lost. But I didn't lose it. The last thing I considered it to be was lost time. I'm sorry I made you think that. Any time I spend with you is fun and worthwhile and wonderful. I want more of it. I don't know how to get it with my schedule, so I'm going to drop my classes."

Jude stared at me. "No, you're not. I didn't spend four hours in the library so you could drop your classes."

"But you're not going to be here much longer—"

"Look." He moved over until we were almost nestled against each other. He touched his fingers to my cheek. "Finish your classes. Study when you need to, and when you don't need to, I'll be here."

"But I study all the time."

"And I understand that. Or I should at least. If we were in Australia, I'd be the one with my nose in a book all the time." He held up his hand as though he was frustrated. "This isn't me, Lys. Well, it is, of course. I haven't been faking having fun, but when I'm in school, all I do is study. Do you know why Shauna and I broke up?"

"Shauna?"

"The girl I told you about. We broke up because studying was more important to me than she was. And I study a lot. Aeronautical engineering isn't basket weaving, you know?"

I smiled. "I know."

"So when I go on holiday, I do nothing but have a good time. You weren't expecting me. I wasn't in your plans. I should have respected what you needed to do."

I shook my head. "I don't even know why you'd want to hang around with me. I'm so boring."

"What are you talking about?"

I held up a finger. "Number One. Rick described me as—what was it? Oh yeah—considerate. What was the other thing? I was dependable? Or loyal? Something that made me sound like a dog."

He chuckled. "It bothered you that he said that."

"A little. It's not very exciting."

"The thing I've found about exciting is that it's like fireworks. A big burst of color. It takes your breath away, and then nothing. But something that's always there, while it might not be as exciting, like the stars in the sky, they can still steal your breath."

The way he was watching me, I thought maybe he wasn't really talking about the stars. My stomach knotted up with the thought that maybe he was referring to me.

"But I've never even left the country. B-O-R-I-N-G."

"That's one perspective, I s'pose."

"You have another?"

"I think I might." He trailed his fingers slowly over my cheek.

"Care to enlighten me?"

He twisted around so he was facing me a little better. "I'm not saying that I'm laughing yet, but the night we met, the way we met, makes for a good story when I get home, and I like good stories. You're fun. You like to go on walks and do extreme sports."

I held up my hand. "One extreme sport."

"All right. One extreme sport. You're daring. Sneaking me into your suite so I can sleep on your couch. Getting me a job so I can have something to eat. Which also shows you're kind. You're brave. We were well and truly lost the other night. You never flinched. I've known girls who would have been crying up a storm. I think you're marvelous. And if Rick didn't see all that, he's an idiot. And if he did see it and still let you go, then he's an even bigger idiot. I'm glad you weren't the one for him, because you deserve the *right* one, not just anyone."

I didn't know what to say to that. I was overwhelmed.

He leaned forward a little more. "It won't bother me at all if you tell me that I'm bloody marvelous, too."

I released an awkward laugh. "You are. You really are. The timing is just . . . I'm confused and I don't want to be. I need to find a way to have my studies and have you in my life, because you're wonderful. Abso-bloody-lutely.

"I think you're fun. You make me smile and laugh. And you're adventuresome. I was only brave the other night because you made me feel safe."

"Do you remember when we were sitting on Mel's bench and I told you there was a girl I loved and she didn't know it?"

"I remember."

"It was you, Lys. You bowled me over, right off. I love you."

I touched his cheek and said to him what I'd

never said to any other guy. Not even Rick. "I love you too."

He grinned. "All right then."

I shook my head, confused. "All right then, what?"

"Then we figure out a way to make this work."

I suddenly felt giddy. He wasn't giving up on me.

"Any ideas?" I asked. "I mean to make it work?"

"I've got a few."

Then he was kissing me. And I was kissing him back.

He put his arms around me, bringing me with him as he lay down on the couch.

Smooth move, Aussie, I thought as I snuggled up against him. *Smooth move.*

"Stephanie called. She'll be back tomorrow," I said.

He reached for the comforter, brought it up over us. "Then tomorrow I'll move back over to Boomer's. Fewer people inconvenienced."

"But for tonight, my couch is your couch."

His arm came around me and held me close.

"I really do think you're wonderful," I said quietly.

He kissed me again.

Maybe eventually we'd move into my bedroom. But for now, I was exactly where I wanted to be, with *the one* I wanted to be with.

For more snow-covered fun,
turn the page to check out an excerpt
of *Snow in Love* by Claire Ray

"Ice cream for lunch. Awesome," Erin said before shoving in two huge mouthfuls.

"Are you going to have any?" Abby asked me.

"No." I looked around the shop, then at each of the tubs sitting in the horizontal cooler. Chocolate, strawberry, vanilla, mint, peanut butter, pistachio, red velvet cake, sweet cream, cookie dough. Nothing looked good. I hoped that being single didn't mean that I'd lost my taste for ice cream!

"How do you feel today?" Erin inquired matter-of-factly.

"Terrible."

Abby reached across and rubbed my shoulder. "At least you have us."

"Yeah," I sighed. "I'm so depressed, I found myself wishing that I had more homework to do."

Erin's face was one of complete horror. "Homework? What?"

"Well, at least it'd be something to do, so that my mind would be occupied."

"Oh, God, you *are* in a bad way."

Erin finished her black licorice mint and pushed the empty cup toward me. "So, I did some digging," she said as I threw her trash away.

"Yeah?" I asked.

"Yeah. Mrs. Stewart was at the front desk this morning and she sure was talkative." She slid forward on her stool, and Abby followed suit.

"You sure you want to hear?"

"How bad is it?"

"Nothing major, just some basic biographical intel."

"Give it to me."

"Evie Stewart. She's eighteen, from Boise, Idaho."

"We knew that already," Abby said.

"How does he know a girl from Idaho anyway?" I stabbed my spoon into my lavender ice cream.

"Her father went to law school with Jake's dad, and they've been friends, like, forever. They've been planning this joint family trip for years."

"For years?" Abby asked, her voice a squeak. I understood what she was asking. She was asking if that meant that Jake and Evie had been dating. For years.

"That rat fink jerk bastard."

Then, the bells attached to the front door

rang out, signaling that my horrible day was about to take a dramatic turn for the worse. In walked Sabrina, Hannah, and Stephanie like three teenaged Minions of Doom. There were few things that could make me feel worse than I already did, but having the unfortunate circumstances of my newfound singledom on display certainly was one of them.

"Hello, girls," my mother welcomed them.

I stood back with my arms crossed while my mother waited on the Minions. I refused to give them any joy, even of the dairy variety.

Once my mother left, Sabrina made a big show of choosing a stool to sit on. Stephanie and Hannah flurried to her side, and together, the three of them pretended to eat their ice cream, while making vicious eyes at me the whole time. I tried to ignore them, and stood by Erin and Abby.

Finally, Sabrina put her spoon down, and began to talk loudly to her two stupid friends about the Northern Lights Ball. "Mom sent me the prettiest pair of shoes to go with my dress. They're blue satin." She looked at me pointedly. "Jessie, do you have your shoes yet?"

Then Stephanie chimed in, "You don't even

have a date anymore, so you won't be able to go, will you?"

Then they burst into laughter. They were still entertaining themselves with conspiratorial laughter when the door opened. At the sight of Will Parker, Sabrina sat taller on her stool. She didn't even try to hide her admiration of him when Cam strolled in after him.

"Hey, Will," Sabrina cooed, "we were just talking about the Northern Lights Ball."

"Yeah?" Will asked.

"Yeah," Sabrina cooed. "You're going, right?"

"I don't know. No date," he said with a giant, gleaming white smile.

Erin quickly looked back and forth between me and Will. I recognized that look. It was the look she got when she was about to come up with a masterly sinister plan.

"You should go with Jessie." Erin's voice got very excited.

"What?" I asked. "No, I'm not going now," I stage-whispered.

"You have to go with somebody! You can't let Jake just go to the dance with that girl and not be there to stop it! And you can't go without a date."

"Will, I don't want to go anymore. So don't worry."

Will took a bite of ice cream and smiled at me. "Come on, Whitman, don't be chicken. I'll take you. It'll be fun."

I didn't know what to say. Everything was happening so fast, I couldn't keep up. I was vaguely aware, though, of how Sabrina and the Minions were staring at me, clearly waiting to hear what I was going to say.

"Okay." I nodded.

"Yeah?" Will asked.

"Yes. It's a date."

Will stood on his stool and high-fived me. "Yeah, Whitman! One date with me and you'll forget all about that guy anyway." He waggled his eyebrows at me. Erin shot a triumphant look at Sabrina, who choked on her bite of ice cream.